HOW

G. LOUISE BEARD

Copyright ©2024 G. Louise Beard

All rights reserved.

ISBN: 978-1-957917-54-2 (paperback)
ISBN: 978-1-957917-55-9 (e-book)

Library of Congress Control Number: 2024916494

All rights reserved. No part of this book may be reproduced, stored in a retrieval system, or transmitted in any form or by any means without prior written permission from the author, except for the use of brief quotations in a book review.

Edited by Vince Font
Cover design by Judith S. Design & Creativity
www.judithsdesign.com
Published by Glass Spider Publishing
www.glassspiderpublishing.com

This book is dedicated to the memory of our parents, Harold and Daisy.

Harold, the son of sharecroppers, was born the eleventh of twelve children. Harold, even though you had only a fourth-grade education, you ensured that each of the five of us (your son and daughters) earned an education beyond high school, with two of us earning post-graduate degrees.

Daisy (Mommy), you started your career as a dessert girl at the hospital where you worked, but after thirty-five years retired as one of the on-site nutritionists.

Thank you both for your guidance and encouragement in working toward taking the steps that allowed us to have the confidence to reach for our goals. Thank you both for guiding us into a Christ-centered faith-based relationship with God.

—*G. Louise Beard*

Chapter 1: A New Beginning

Standing outside the storefront offices of the new law firm of Jackson and Monroe Attorneys-at-Law, Bailey Anderson looked through the window and surveyed the small three-room workplace. She smiled and thought to herself that this was going to be the perfect work environment for her.

As a newly graduated office manager for two young and eager attorneys who had just passed their bar exams and completed their internships a year earlier, Bailey felt truly blessed. She was convinced there was not a more perfect place than here for her to start her career as an executive assistant.

When Bailey saw movement inside, she stepped to the door and walked through. She quickly noticed the two men who were now her bosses. The shorter of the two, Alexander Jackson, the man who'd hired her, was standing with another man who looked at her as if she was interrupting something important.

She smiled at them and cheerfully said, "Good morning, gentlemen. Mr. Jackson, I hope I'm not too late."

"No, Miss Anderson," Mr. Jackson replied, "you're not late at all. We like to get here early just to have some time to ourselves before the rush begins. Let me show you around and explain the situation to you."

The second man, Mr. Jackson's partner, Xavier Monroe, did not speak and continued looking at Bailey as though she was an intruder he wished would go away. Feeling somewhat uneasy, Bailey gave the intense man a half-smile and turned to follow Mr. Jackson.

After her first six weeks, things in the office began to fall into a routine. Bailey managed to get to the office by 7:00 sharp every morning. When she arrived, she began her daily routine of preparing the coffee for the first of three pots throughout the day. Then she would review the case notes from the day before and make adjustments to the schedules for her employers. Finally, she started working on the business for the day. Usually by 8:30 when the partners came in, Bailey had everything under control and would hand each their appointment lists, client summaries, and their first cup of black coffee for the day.

After her first six months, Bailey was certain this was going to be a good working environment. She was getting to know some things about the partners. She learned that Alexander Jackson was married and loved his wife very much. She came to the understanding that Mr. Jackson was an open-minded, easygoing person who made others feel welcome. Every morning, he made a point to ask Bailey how she was feeling and if there was anything special that needed to be done for her.

His wife, Melody, had been the receptionist/secretary until they found out she was expecting. After the baby's first birthday, Melody planned to start using her teachers' certificate to give them a financial cushion until the law offices expanded. Mr. Jackson was strait-laced and conservative; he looked like a family man.

Xavier Monroe, on the other hand, was guarded and restrained. He seldom spoke to Bailey, and when he did, it was all business. He was reserved and never asked her anything personal like how she felt or if she'd had a good weekend. He was composed and businesslike with his clients. He wasn't one to waste words. He had four suits, in contrast to Mr. Jackson's two, and he always looked crisp and fresh. Xavier Monroe was debonair, refined, and well-groomed, but he worked hard at being indifferent and unemotional. It became apparent to Bailey that Xavier Monroe was a snob, and he wore it like a badge of honor.

Even with their distinct personality traits, the work environment was a good one. The office was bright, well-lit, had a professional atmosphere, and was easy to keep clean. Bailey thought it was nice to have that big window to look out and see what was happening throughout the day, especially since she was the only other person in the office besides the attorneys and there were times when they were both gone and she had nothing to do.

After four years of working hard at building a good reputation, the workload for the attorneys was getting heavier. Bailey had no complaints; she didn't like to create things to do to look busy. As a result of the increased business, the attorneys had to add another phone line, hire a part-time receptionist, and expand the capabilities of their computer system. Things were looking good for Jackson and Monroe Attorneys-at-Law.

Chapter 2: Moving on Up

One morning in her fifth year at Jackson and Monroe, Bailey found herself hurrying to work. The bus was late because of an accident, and she'd lost thirty minutes from her schedule. She still had a few more files that needed to be packed before the movers arrived. Today of all days there had to be problems. The offices of Jackson and Monroe were relocating. The attorneys needed more room. They had taken on a law clerk and another associate, added a permanent receptionist, and today was moving day.

Getting off the bus, Bailey almost ran down the street toward the office. When she pushed through the door, the attorneys were standing shoulder to shoulder, looking at her.

She took a deep breath. "I'm so sorry I'm late. There was an accident, and the bus was caught up in the traffic jam. I'm so sorry!" After closing her eyes and taking a few breaths, she slowly opened her eyes. Looking around, she realized no one was saying anything, but they were all smiling at her.

Taking in everything and everyone around her, Bailey saw that Melody Jackson and little Alex Jr. were in the office. *What are they doing here?* she wondered. Then she saw that Ja'Nell, the receptionist, was standing with a very distinguished-looking older couple, and everyone had a cup in their hands.

"Surprise! Happy anniversary!" everyone shouted.

Ja'Nell, the office receptionist, offered Bailey a cup of ginger ale. "Congratulations on your fifth year at Jackson and Monroe," the young woman said.

Even Xavier Monroe pushed aside his usual stoic manner and congratulated Bailey. He then introduced the older couple as his parents, Judge Melvin C. and Mrs. Helen Monroe.

Judge Monroe, Bailey thought. *No wonder he's so reserved.* It was now very clear to her that Xavier was a carbon copy of his father, the Honorable Judge Melvin C. Monroe, one of the most respectfully feared criminal judges on the federal court of appeals.

As they were greeting one another, Mrs. Monroe interrupted Bailey's thoughts. "Hello, young lady, it's such a pleasure to finally meet you. You need to know that you have been a lifesaver for Jackson and Monroe."

At that point, Judge Monroe spoke up. "Helen, don't tell her anything like that, she may believe that she should get a raise along with the praise." Then he took Mrs. Monroe's elbow and led her across the room. Before Bailey could react to the judge's comment, Ja'Nell announced that the moving van had arrived, and the fun of loading and unloading began.

The new offices were across town in a more affluent business district. The offices were spacious and well-designed. The lighting was soft, the floors were fully carpeted, and the walls were covered with matching elegant wallpaper. There was an intercom system with the capability to play low-key music in the reception/waiting room area. The best part of the new location, for Bailey, was that there was an administrative center for her that overlooked the reception area. It gave easy access to the lawyers' offices and was close to the law library and the conference rooms.

All in all, the move was wonderful. Bailey and Ja'Nell spent several days organizing the materials and setting up the offices for business. Getting all the books on the shelves in the legal library was a major task, so it was left for last.

By the end of the week, there was nothing Bailey could think of other than getting home and staying put for the next two days.

* * *

Home at last. It was nine o'clock Friday night, and Bailey was just getting home. But it was worth it; she had taken care of her business. Now she could have the weekend to herself. She unlocked the door to her apartment and practically fell through the opening into the entryway. Her aching arms were full of bags and packages. "This is for the birds. I have got to get a car!" Bailey exclaimed. "This traveling by public transportation is really getting to me!"

She stumbled to the kitchen to unpack her shopping bags and began putting the groceries away. Then she went to the linen closet and put away her toiletries. Finally, she started running the water for a much-desired bubble bath.

Just as she settled up to her shoulders in bubbles and warm water, the phone rang. "Oh, who could that be? Well, they can leave a message. I need this downtime."

An hour later, she was stepping out of the bathroom and dressing in her favorite pajamas and fuzzy slippers when her doorbell began to ring persistently. Grabbing her robe, she rushed to the door and looked through the vantage point.

Mr. Monroe! Oh, my goodness, what is he doing here? she wondered.

As Bailey opened the door, Xavier Monroe pushed his way in.

"Where have you been? I've been calling you all evening! Don't you check your messages?"

She couldn't believe her ears or her eyes. Did her boss just indignantly push his way into her apartment interrupting her quiet time and making persistent inquiries?

"Mr. Monroe, what can I do for you?" Bailey asked quizzically. "Is something wrong?"

"Yes, something is wrong!" he retorted. "Do you think that I would have been calling you or that I would even be here if something wasn't wrong?"

Bailey was getting a little vexed. "Well, what do you want? Did I neglect to complete some depositions for you?"

"No, nothing like that! I need your help. I know that it's last minute, but I really need your help! My parents usually host a wine and cheese reception every year, but this year they are going on a cruise, and I have been asked to host the celebration."

Bailey looked at him. "And?"

"And," Xavier said, "I need you to get the party organized and to host it with me!"

Bailey was stunned. "What? Are you kidding? When is it?" Was he really asking her to help him do something not related to the office work—something in the social realm?

Handing her a box, he said, "You have five weeks. Here's the list of guests and the wines and cheeses that you need to order as soon as possible. Do a good job and don't embarrass me. My parents have been hosting this event for twenty years, so make this an elegant affair, and don't let them down."

With that done, Xavier Monroe turned on his heel and walked out of Bailey's apartment, leaving her astonished.

Was he really serious? That took some nerve. Bailey started to go after him before he could get on the elevator, but not being one to cause a scene, she let him go. What was she going to do?

There was only one thing to do—call the Judge and Mrs. Monroe and ask for some instruction.

That was exactly what she did early the next morning. Mrs. Monroe was surprised but arranged to meet Bailey and give her the already printed invitations, offer some recommendations, and have a small lunch.

"Miss Anderson, my son is too serious for his own good," Helen Monroe declared when they met at the restaurant.

She further explained that Xavier didn't understand everything related to the annual fundraiser was always arranged a year in advance and that he was only expected to be the host this year.

"Now, these are the invitations and the stamped envelopes. Just stuff them and mail them by Monday afternoon. I've also given you a copy of this year's program. Everything that needs to be done has been arranged. However, if you feel so inclined, go ahead and make some changes to the program just to give it your personal touch. It's been the same for quite a few years, a simple 'meet, greet, give me the check, eat, and go home' agenda. And despite my son's uptight attitude, I think you will make a beautiful and gracious hostess."

With that said, Mrs. Monroe brightened and said, "Now, young lady, let's have something to eat. I love the offerings at this restaurant."

Bailey smiled gratefully. "Thank you for your help. And yes, I agree. Let's enjoy some delicious food."

After a light lunch and getting to know one another a little more, Bailey gathered the materials, Mrs. Monroe paid the bill, and they parted company.

HOW

* * *

Sunday afternoon was a quiet day, so Bailey decided it was a great time to research hosting a wine and cheese reception. She surrounded herself with the latest home entertainment magazines and viewed several websites. She learned a lot, but she thought one of the most important things to do included having a reception line to greet each guest personally. She also decided keeping the atmosphere light would add to the success of the reception. Now all she had to do was find a way to create a mood that was encouraging and upbeat without being overbearing and pretentious.

Because this event was a fundraiser for the children's wing of Benton General Hospital, Bailey wanted it to be a successful venture, and she wanted to make an impression on her boss and his family, as well.

Chapter 3: Being Insolent

That Monday morning, while Bailey was going about her daily office preparation routine, Xavier Monroe walked into the administration area. "So, what have you done and what do you have left to do?" he asked her.

Bailey slowly turned to face him. "Good morning, Mr. Monroe. Did you have a pleasant weekend?"

She didn't have to tell Xavier Monroe that she had everything under control. He was such a pushy snob. She would let him sweat for a few moments at least.

Xavier appeared taken aback but quickly recovered, and without acknowledging her inquiry, he asked her the question again. Once more, she ignored his query.

"Mr. Monroe, I would love to chat with you, but right now I'm in the middle of my office preparations and don't have time to talk. Maybe when I have a quick break I'll stop by your office." She smiled pleasantly and walked into the library to shelve a few books.

Xavier had never been treated that way before.

Who does she think she is? he thought. *I've never met anyone so insolent in my life.*

But what could he do? He was asking her to step beyond her

duties at the office and do something for him on a nonprofessional and purely social scale.

It wasn't until 4:30 in the afternoon, as he was returning from a child custody case, that Bailey followed him to his office. She knocked softly on his office door, stepped inside, and informed him of what plans she had implemented and what plans remained to be instituted for the fundraiser.

"Well, see that you get those things done as soon as possible. We don't want to wait until the last minute and have this thing look like an amateur organized the affair."

Trying not to let it show on her face, Bailey thought, *I am an amateur, and you knew that when you threw this into my lap.* But instead of saying that out loud, she smiled tightly and said, "Good night, Mr. Monroe."

* * *

The night before the twenty-first annual Benton General Hospital children's fundraiser, Bailey Anderson arrived at the hospital's rotunda right after work to check out the decorations. Everything looked better than she'd expected. She had decorated theme tables that were to be hosted by men and women dressed in costumes representative of children's heroes.

Because every detail was in place, all she had to do that evening was to place the cards on the tables throughout the room for the caterers and leave the list of songs for the disc jockey to play between the sets of the stringed instrument ensemble.

One of the helpful suggestions she'd gotten from the etiquette books was to create a mood for the occasion, and as she looked around, that was what she had done. She wanted this to be a celebration instead of an obligation for the guests. There was even a small dance floor in front of the stage where the musicians would be seated in case anyone wanted to enjoy the music.

Bailey had also contacted the department store managers and business owners throughout the greater downtown area. To her joy and delight, she found that they were more than pleased to be asked to participate in and donate to the children's hospital fundraiser.

Bailey's plans even included a gift for each of the two hundred invited guests. The gift was an Asian-designed silk bag. In each bag were trial-sized containers of hair care products, body and facial moisturizers, lotions and body butters, store coupons, gift cards, perfume and cologne samples, small boxes of European chocolates, and an engraved pledge/thank-you card signed by Judge and Mrs. Monroe.

Chapter 4: Let's Party

On the morning of the fundraiser, Bailey woke up startled. She had been so busy with the arrangements that she hadn't given a thought to what she would wear.

It would be great if I had a special dress and a different hairstyle, she thought to herself.

Just then, she bounded out of bed and ran to her closet. There was that dress she'd gotten on clearance six months ago. She had bought it on a whim. It was so beautiful that she couldn't leave it in the store. Finally, tonight, she would get a chance to wear it.

Next, she had to take care of her hair. It had been a while since her last professional styling, and it was too late to get an appointment, so she had to take her chances and do it herself.

Later that afternoon, with one final look at herself in the full-length mirror behind her bedroom door, Bailey shrugged into her fake fur jacket, picked up her tote bag that contained her silver shoes and matching purse, and walked out of her apartment. She arrived at the rotunda two hours before the event was to start.

Not wanting the caterers and musicians to feel like she was being intrusive and fussy, Bailey kept her distance and only spoke to them when asked a question, or when she was asked to give her approval for something. The room looked amazing; an atmosphere of celebration and festivity was all around.

Xavier Monroe arrived thirty minutes before the start of the reception. He looked around and quickly approached Bailey. "I need to speak to you, Miss Anderson," he said and took her by the arm, almost dragging her to the stage area. "What is this? It looks like a carnival in here! I knew I'd made a mistake trusting you. I should have gotten a professional to do this."

Bailey snatched her arm from Xavier's grasp. "Well, you didn't, and this is what you got. So just kindly get away from me. You're such an ungrateful stuffed shirt." She hadn't meant to speak to him the way she did, but she was taken aback by his attitude. "You came to me and dumped this on me with no instructions and offered no help. Now here you are at the very last minute with complaints and words of discontent. How dare you!"

Xavier stepped to her with a scowl on his face. "Listen, young lady, who do you think you're speaking to? I trusted you with this affair, and now I see that you've made a mess of the whole thing."

"You don't know how this is going to work out," Bailey retorted. "It hasn't even started yet. And *you*," she said, stabbing her finger into his shoulder, "are part of the reception line, so go over to the door and do your job!"

She turned and quickly walked away, positioning herself at the end of the receiving line, where she handed a gift bag to each guest and informed them of the pledge card in the bag's outer pocket. During planning, she thought that being given the cards would take the pressure off the patrons to make a donation on the spot and free them to enjoy themselves.

After all of the invited guests had arrived, Bailey stood on the stage and addressed the crowd. "Good evening, everyone. I'm Bailey Anderson, your co-host for this evening, and I would like to welcome you all to the twenty-first annual fundraiser for the Benton General Hospital's children's wing."

The guests clapped politely and once they stopped, she continued confidently with her introduction, trying not to let her nervousness be known.

"I would like to say thanks to all who were involved in organizing the event, to all who are serving tonight, and especially the greater downtown merchants and business owners who donated the gifts for tonight. And finally, to you, our guests. Thank you for coming. Please relax and enjoy the evening, and don't forget that after you've filled out your pledge cards, you should deposit them in the golden urn at the door. Thank you again, everyone, and have a wonderful evening."

For the rest of the night, Bailey played cat and mouse with Xavier Monroe. At one point, he caught up with her while she was redirecting some of the wine servers. "You can't run from me all night, Miss Anderson."

She looked at him and gave him a sweet, sugary smile. "Oh, really? Well, watch this," she said and scurried off again to another part of the rotunda to converse with several groups of guests.

As Xavier watched her walk away, it was his turn to smile. Bailey was feisty and challenging. Against his better judgment, Xavier had to admit that the affair was a total success—that was, if he could go by the comments he'd overheard as he strolled around the room:

"How absolutely interesting!"

"This is actually fun this year."

"Can you believe that there's no pressure to present our contributions tonight?"

"I wonder if I can get that Anderson girl to organize our Christmas and New Year's occasions this year."

"Wait until I tell Melvin and Helen what they missed."

"That girl is a jewel. Is she a professional organizer?"

Finally, it was two o'clock in the morning and the rotunda was being restored to its usual appearance. The musicians, the disc jockey, and the caterers packed up while Bailey retrieved the pledge cards from the golden urn and filed them in a box alphabetically. The last duty of the night was to give the final checks to the wait staff, caterers, and musicians, after which she was more than ready to go home.

I'm so tired, Bailey thought. *Good thing it's Friday. I'm sleeping in for the rest of the weekend. I sure hope I can get a cab this time of night.*

Then she smiled and gave a little chuckle.

Maybe I should say 'this time of the morning.' If I wait another hour or two, I can catch the bus home.

It was, in fact, another hour before everyone exited the rotunda and Bailey went looking for a taxi. Suddenly, a shadow overtook her. "Surely you have a ride. I know you aren't thinking about getting a cab this time of the morning."

Before she could answer him, Xavier relieved her of the box of cards and started walking toward the parking lot. He called back to her, "Well, don't just stand there, get in the car so we can get this night over with."

Chapter 5: Apology

Something made Bailey open her eyes. She thought maybe she was having a bad dream. Looking around the semi-dark room, she listened to the sounds of peaceful quiet as she lay there wondering what it could have been. Then she heard something. What was that noise, and why wouldn't it stop? She rolled over and realized someone was ringing her doorbell and persistently knocking on the door. She sat up quickly, put on her robe and slippers, and hastily made her way through the apartment to her door. As she stumbled into the entryway, she called out, "Who is it?"

"Miss Anderson, open the door!" a voice said.

Bailey pushed her hair out of her eyes and looked through the peephole. It was Xavier Monroe. "Oh, now what?" she whispered to herself. She cracked the door and looked out through the slender opening. "What can I do for you, Mr. Monroe?"

"Like I said, open the door," came his reply, but before she could, he pushed his way into the apartment and closed the door behind him. "Are you still in the bed? It's two o'clock in the afternoon."

"Mr. Monroe, what can I do for you, please?" Bailey was still groggy from having been awakened in such an abrupt manner, and it was hard for her to focus. "Just have a seat," she said as she walked down the hall to her bedroom, grabbed some clothes, and went into the bathroom to take a quick shower and get herself together.

When she returned to the living room, her boss stood up. "Well, you look much better. Now get your coat so we can go. We have to send out the pledge cards and start collecting the money."

"Mr. Monroe, that's not necessary. Those pledge cards were printed on NCR paper and the guest copy folds into a pre-addressed envelope. So we have about two weeks before all of the pledges are due."

"So you think you've covered all the bases, huh?" Xavier snapped scornfully. "Well, what address did you put on the envelopes?"

Bailey informed him that she used the organization's PO box like she was instructed to do by his mother. "And since your parents will have returned from their cruise by then," she added, "I have no other obligations to the fundraiser. My job is done." She walked to her apartment door and opened it. "Now if that's all, thanks for coming, and have a good weekend, Mr. Monroe."

Xavier stepped over to her. "Not so fast, young lady. My mother commanded me to take you to lunch today to thank you for doing such a good job. So get your coat, and let's get this over with."

Bailey shook her head. "If you don't mind, I'll pass. I'm too tired to go anywhere. I'm going back to bed. We can do this some other time."

Reaching around her, he closed the door again. "No, either we do it now or we don't do it at all."

With one hand on the doorknob and the other hand on her hip, she opened the door again. Xavier looked at her and then at the door. After a moment of clarity, he hunched his shoulders, said, "Suit yourself!" and walked out, slamming the door behind him.

* * *

By the time Monday morning came around, Bailey was rested and ready to go back to work. She had a spring in her step and was feeling somewhat gratified. As she stepped off the bus and approached the Jackson and Monroe Attorneys-at-Law building, she smiled at the memory that Mr. Monroe had told her his mother thought she did a good job.

Since meeting her and having lunch with her, she found she liked Helen Monroe, and in view of the fact she'd spent so much of her free time working on the fundraiser, Bailey had developed a respect for the stately-looking, unflappable lady with the kind smile and gracious attitude.

Too bad I don't feel the same way about her uptight, pigheaded, snobbish son! she thought.

When she opened the doors of the offices and stepped into the reception area, Bailey detected the scent of fresh flowers. The scent was heavy and intoxicating and permeated the air.

Walking closer to her office, the scent became stronger, and when she entered the space, she immediately saw the source of the scent. The area was filled with six large vases containing dozens of roses in various colors. The arrangements occupied every available surface in her office.

Each bouquet of roses had a card extending from the vase that read *Thank you*, and each named a specific item: *for the delicious food; for the wonderful music; for including the downtown merchants; for the entertaining atmosphere; for all of your hard work.*

After the inspection, Bailey went to her desk to put her purse away and found a five-pound box of assorted European chocolates propped on her desk. There was a note taped to the top of the chocolate box. It read *Miss Anderson: I wanted to thank you for doing such an outstanding job on the fundraiser. It was a huge success. My parents tell me that their email boxes were filled with praises about the affair and you. Many of the patrons were very impressed with the presentation of the event. Also, you were an outstanding hostess. Thank you again, Xavier Monroe*

Bailey never expected anything like this. It was very nice. It set the pace for the whole day. When Ja'Nell arrived, she was in awe. "Wow, Miss Bailey, what is all this?"

Before settling down to start working, Ja'Nell moved from one vase to the other, deeply inhaling the aroma of each enormous bouquet. She read each card and then read the thank-you note on the box of chocolates. "This is so nice. Looks like you made an impression on the Iceman. Congratulations, girl."

Bailey let herself smile. "Yeah, well, it's over now, and this is all very nice, but we have work to do today. The partners are out of the office for the entire day, and the two associates won't be in until after their court proceedings are over. So let's get busy, young lady, and maybe we can let you go home early today."

During the lunch hour, a courier came into the office with a small package that required a signature. It was addressed to Bailey. When she opened the envelope, she found a small box with a key fob to an automobile in it. The note that accompanied the fob read: *In stall number 2-11 in the parking garage is a car that has been leased for you. Enjoy it.*

She must have looked very strange because Ja'Nell ran to her. "Miss Bailey! What is it? What's wrong? Are you okay?" Bailey handed her the note, and Ja'Nell screamed. "Well, don't just stand there, girl, let's go see what it looks like!"

Taking the elevator to the parking garage, Bailey stepped out and immediately noticed several security guards standing near a car adorned with a huge bright-red ribbon. Benny, the captain, called, "Hey there, young lady! I understand this is for you. Get over here and see what you got!"

Parked right there in stall number 2-11 was an Audi A4 sedan in Manhattan gray with muted gold highlights and a creamy, muted cranberry red interior.

"What's the matter with you, Miss Bailey?" Ja'Nell said. "Why are you just standing there? Oh...you can't drive, can you? Ooh, you don't have a license, do you?" Ja'Nell's comments set off a torrent of questions about Bailey's driving abilities and whether she was a licensed driver or not.

"Calm down, calm down, everybody. Of course I can drive, and yes, I do have a license. Mr. Benny, you know that because you've seen me in those rental cars I get sometimes."

She took another minute to stare at the car. She walked around it, touched the mirrors and the lights, and after all of that, she touched the button on the remote key bar and opened the door. She sat in the driver's seat and looked around the inner recesses of the vehicle.

"This is a beautiful car," she said. Then, to herself, she thought, *It's so plush. Why did he do this? It's too much!*

She exited the vehicle, locked the door, and walked back to the elevator, calling back over her shoulder, "Okay, now, everyone. Let's get back to work. This is nice, but it's still just a car, and we all have some work to do."

She stepped into the elevator and held it for Ja'Nell. They rode back to the fifth-floor offices of Jackson and Monroe in silence.

The rest of the day was nerve-racking for Bailey because she was torn about what to do. Number one: She couldn't accept that car. *But* just a few weeks ago she'd said that she needed to get a car because it was so challenging using public transportation all the time. Number two: Having a car *would* make it easier to get around; sometimes she spent the whole day on buses, in taxi cabs, waiting for someone to pick her up, or just waiting in line to get a rental. Number three: There was one thing for sure…that car was a little too upscale for her. *But* she wasn't footing the bill, and it *would* be convenient for her to just walk out of her apartment and get in the car instead of standing at the bus stop. The best part was that for a year, she could leave an hour and a half later than usual and still get to work on time.

Ja'Nell helped Bailey carry four of the vases of roses to the car at the end of the day. When she offered Ja'Nell a ride, the young assistant accepted readily. As they rode through the city, they talked. At Ja'Nell's insistence, Bailey described the events of the fundraiser as well as the ride home in Xavier Monroe's car, including his visit to her apartment the following day.

"It sounds like everything was perfect," Ja'Nell said. "Although you weren't very nice to the Iceman in not taking him up on his lunch offer. It's still no wonder you got all this good stuff today."

When she dropped Ja'Nell off, Bailey insisted she take one of the bouquets of roses. Bailey had no idea where she was going to put the other three, but on the way home she decided it would be nice to wake up and see them in the morning, so she placed one on the dresser in her bedroom, one on the table in her little entryway, and the other in the center of her coffee table where she would see them as she entered her apartment. She deposited the box of chocolates in her refrigerator. She would bag them and freeze them later.

Chapter 6: Using a Newfound Talent

Things at the office began to fall back into a routine within a week, but Bailey found her evenings to be quite full. She had received several requests to be a party planner—better yet, an *events coordinator*—from some of the patrons at the hospital fundraiser.

To add to her full plate, the holiday season was coming, and Bailey had been contacted by a member of the local chamber of commerce and asked to organize two holiday affairs to be held in the downtown municipal building. The first was to be held two weeks after Thanksgiving; the other was a New Year's Eve celebration.

This time, she recruited Ja'Nell to be her assistant. Together they worked several nights a week after work and most weekends, usually at Bailey's apartment. Planning, advertising, and making all the necessary arrangements was fun, at least most of the time, and Bailey had even found new dresses and got her hair styled for these occasions.

To say that the chamber of commerce Christmas party was

elegant and original would be an understatement. The colors were shimmering red and gold. Bailey had the servers dressed like the ancient kings of the Orient. The champagne flowed freely, the finger foods were flawless, and the music was stimulating and moving. The entertainment was provided by several high-school choirs and drama clubs, and the occasion was enjoyable and amusing.

The New Year's Eve party was even more astonishing. The favors were unusual and the food, as before, was memorable. The music was a big hit with a combination of old favorites from the 1950s, 60s, and 70s.

Everyone had a great time, and many of the guests were pleasantly surprised when a designated driver service was made available to those who were "slightly and more" inebriated. The president of the chamber of commerce was so pleased that he gave Bailey a bonus, which turned out to be two hundred dollars above their agreed-upon fee.

The final goodbyes were made at three o'clock in the morning, and after dropping Ja'Nell off at her parents' house, Bailey headed home. As she drove, she had a conversation with herself.

I really need to thank Mr. Monroe again for this car, Bailey thought. *It's been a lifesaver these last couple of months. After the lease period is over, I'll really have to buy a car.*

She drove a little farther then chuckled to herself.

"Well, Miss Bailey," she said aloud, smiling broadly, "I guess you've let yourself get spoiled, girl."

By the time she pulled into her parking space in the apartment parking lot, she was so tired she had to concentrate on her every step. Once inside, she began to shed her clothes, leaving a trail of shoes, her coat, dress, slip, and pantyhose. Exhausted, she collapsed onto her bed and immediately fell asleep.

HOW

* * *

It was 1:45 in the afternoon on New Year's Day, and Bailey was just getting up. She settled into her bathtub for a long soak, but just as she was starting to enjoy the silky feel of the water and the soothing aroma of the lavender chamomile-scented bath oil, the phone rang.

"Hello," she croaked into the receiver.

"I guess you're still in bed," the voice on the other end remarked. "Do you ever do anything but sleep?"

"Hello, Mr. Monroe. For your information, if it's even any of your business, I'm not still in bed. What can I do for you today?"

"Good. I'll be there in forty-five minutes. Be ready," he said and broke the connection.

Reluctantly cutting her bath short, Bailey was ready by the time her employer arrived. She opened the door and was surprised to see Xavier dressed down in a pair of slacks and a jacket. "Well, here you are," she said. "Where are we going?"

Xavier looked her up and down and actually smiled. "You look nice for someone who got home at 3:55 in the morning. We are going to eat. For me, it will be lunch; for you, it will undoubtedly be breakfast."

While they were driving to the restaurant, Bailey asked, "How do you know what time I got home?"

"I was just guessing," he replied. "When were you going to tell me that you were moonlighting as a party planner?"

"That's an events coordinator, thank you very much, and I really wasn't planning on telling you at all. What I do before or after work is really none of your concern. When do you ever tell me your personal business?" Bailey was trying to keep her voice light, but she was anxious and uneasy about the conversation.

"Oh, you're a little uncomfortable, aren't you?" Xavier remarked. "I bet you think I've been spying on you. Well, rest assured, I have not been following you. I'm not a stalker. I actually have a life. As you know, my parents were guests at the party last night, and they heard some of the other guests talking about how they were impressed with your party planning skills—first with the children's hospital fundraiser and now with the chamber of commerce events. Imagine my surprise at finding out that you were the...*events coordinator*. Then my mother asked me if I had taken you to lunch yet. I told her we hadn't had the opportunity to have lunch together, so here we are. It's no big deal. I'm simply keeping my promise to my dear mother."

Surprisingly, the conversation over lunch was pleasant, amiable, and almost cheerful. Bailey and Xavier talked like two people just getting to know each other. When the meal was over, they walked the footpath through the park, looked at the sights, and did some light shopping. By early evening, they were each ready to call it a day.

"I had a really nice time today," Xavier said as he walked Bailey to the door of her apartment. "It's been quite a while since I've spent time doing the proverbial laid-back things that people do on the weekends and holidays. I would like to do it again sometime if that's alright with you."

Bailey was a bit taken aback by his request, but she flashed a smile and nodded her head. "Yes, that would be nice. Thank you. Have a good night," she said as she stepped through the entryway and slowly closed the door.

Once she was alone, she whispered to herself, mimicking Xavier. "I'd like to do this again." She took off her jacket and walked to her bedroom. "I wonder what he's up to. Why would he want to date me?" she voiced out loud. "I know him. He doesn't do anything without having a reason."

She turned and looked back in the direction of her front door, putting her hands on her hips. "Just what *are* you up to, Mr. Monroe?"

Chapter 7: Talents Revealed

Bailey continued to work evenings and weekends as an events coordinator. As she had with the chamber of commerce events, she recruited Ja'Nell to be her assistant.

It became the norm for Bailey and Ja'Nell to find themselves working three out of four weekends every month. In addition to working large events, they also began to take on smaller, more intimate gatherings. It was all fun and getting to be very profitable. After six months, Bailey had enough money in reserve to pay for her small business license, and she was saving up to buy her own car. Yet with all of the time spent on the party and reception planning plus her daily responsibilities at the law offices, Bailey felt as if things were getting a bit out of control.

Noticing that her usual exuberance was waning, Xavier stopped Bailey one evening as the offices were closing. "Miss Anderson," he asked, "is something wrong? You don't seem to be yourself lately."

Bailey hadn't heard him approach, and she spun around quickly. "Oh! Good evening, Mr. Monroe. You startled me. I thought everyone was gone for the night. And to answer your inquiry, nothing is wrong. I'm just a little fatigued. Too many late nights planning and attending parties and social events."

It was Xavier who came up with a solution to the problem when he suggested that Bailey set up a real office and hire a part-time employee to manage the office and organize the dates for the parties and other events. He even offered to help her with the legal requirements for the official incorporation of a small business so that things would progress nicely with much less stress.

As it turned out, there was a small office in a storefront building two blocks away from the Jackson and Monroe offices. Bailey was also fortunate that her mother, Bertha Anderson, agreed to be her part-time employee. Having recently retired and discovered she wasn't a stay-at-home-all-day person, Bertha was more than happy to have something to do.

Every morning, mother and daughter would ride to work together, and at four o'clock every afternoon, Bertha would close the office and take the bus home. She was content with the arrangements and enjoyed her duties. Bailey's new business, Classic Party Planners, was reaping the benefits of Bertha Anderson's outstanding managerial and clerical skills.

Chapter 8: A Favor

Bailey's birthday was June 4th. This year, it fell on a Monday, and by the time she got to the office, she had made up her mind that she was going to gift herself with her very own car.

"Happy Birthday, Miss Bailey," Ja'Nell said, holding a small box in her hands. "I hope that this is one of your happiest birthdays."

"Thank you," she said, "but you shouldn't have spent your hard-earned money on me. Aren't you saving to move into your own apartment?"

"I sure am," Ja'Nell said, "and thanks to your letting me work for you, I'm just about ready to make my move. Please let me spend a little something on you?"

The ladies hugged, and when Bailey opened the box, she lifted a large multicolored silk scarf from the tissue paper. She smiled and put it around her neck. "Oh, this is so beautiful! Thank you, Ja'Nell."

At the end of the day, Bailey shut down the computers, checked the doors, and put the phones on stand-by. On her final check, she noticed the light was still on in Xavier's office, so she knocked on the door.

She was surprised when she heard Xavier say, "Yes? Come in."

She opened the door. "I'm sorry, Mr. Monroe, I wasn't aware you were still here. I'm just closing the office, and I saw your light. I didn't know you were working late. Good night."

As she was backing out of the office, Xavier called to her, "Miss Anderson, just one moment." He stood and walked to the door. "Today is your birthday, isn't it?" Bailey smiled slightly and nodded her head. Then Xavier asked, "Do you have any plans?"

Feeling self-conscious, Bailey shook her head. "Not right now, but I am going to buy myself a car. Tomorrow is the target day for the one I've been driving. I'm going to turn it in early and start looking for one that I can afford to buy. I've gotten pretty spoiled not having to take public transportation everywhere I go."

"Well," Xavier said, "I'm glad that we got this chance to talk because I have something for you." He beckoned her into the office, reached into the stationary drawer of his desk, and took out an envelope. "Happy birthday, Miss Anderson, I hope you enjoy this."

She took the envelope and opened it. "Is this what I think it is? Oh, no. I can't let you do this. It's too much." The envelope contained the title to the Audi A4 sedan.

"Well, it's already done, so you have to accept it." he voiced softly as he smiled.

Bailey looked at her employer and noted to herself that even though it was something that he rarely did, smiling looked good on him. He had a beautiful smile. It made his handsome face light up. She found herself smiling too. "I guess I could accept it because I've actually gotten really attached to that car."

"Good! Now that it's settled, go home, and I'll pick you up in an hour. Let's go to dinner."

* * *

Things went cordially over dinner, but Xavier seemed preoccupied. "Mr. Monroe," Bailey asked, "is something wrong?"

"No," he replied, "not really." Then he cleared his throat and leaned forward. "Miss Anderson…I'm sorry I'm not good company tonight. Let me take you home, and we can do this again some other time."

"Mr. Monroe, we have been associated with one another for seven years now. I can read your moods most of the time. And right now, I can tell something is bothering you. What is it?"

Xavier sighed. "Okay, then, little Miss Mind Reader, if you must know. It's really not a problem. My father told me that I'm being considered for a position in the state's district attorney's office. He thinks I have a good chance of getting an appointment, but my being single could be a detriment. He says it could be construed as a weakness or a flaw in my personality. It makes me look unsettled, and that could lead to problems for the person who will serve as the state's top attorney."

Bailey looked at him for a moment before responding. "Well, then, why don't you get engaged? I'm sure you have someone in your life who would be a good wife and help you achieve your goals in life."

He looked at her and offered a half-smile, reached across the table, and took her hand. "Miss Anderson, you are unbelievable."

* * *

On Friday afternoon, Xavier sent a message to Bailey through the interoffice text message system. He asked her to stay at the office for an hour longer because he wanted to meet with her. His lunch meeting had run late, and he would be back at the offices soon.

Bailey didn't mind. There was a decree of divorce that had to be amended for Mr. Jackson. *One less thing to do on Monday morning,* she thought to herself.

When Xavier finally arrived, he looked apprehensive as he walked into the administration office and stood across the desk, looking at Bailey.

"Hello, Mr. Monroe," she said, looking up. "You're right on time. I'm just shutting down the computer. What did you need?"

He leaned across her desk and said, "I've been thinking about what you said Monday at dinner. You know, about getting engaged. I want to ask you a favor... Be my fiancée."

"What?" Bailey exclaimed. "Are you kidding? Wait a minute, you've been drinking. Oh, no. You need to go home and sober up."

Bailey wondered what was going on with her boss. She couldn't believe he had overindulged. It was not like him. He was usually so uptight and disciplined that she couldn't believe he ever did anything as impulsive and rash as getting drunk.

"I'm not drunk. I just had two little drinks. No, maybe it was three or four." Waving his hand, he impatiently asserted, "Whatever. So are you going to say yes?" He stumbled back a couple of steps and chuckled. "Oops. I think I may have had one too many."

Bailey ran to take his arm before he could fall over. "Okay, big boy, let's go get you sobered up."

She picked up her purse and keys. Then, claiming his arm, she guided him out of the office. By the time they got to the parking garage, Bailey knew Xavier was in no condition to drive, so she kept hold of his arm and led him to her car.

"You're drunk, and I'm not about to let you drive," she

informed him. "You're coming home with me."

In the car Xavier, continued to lay out his course of action. "We can start going out regularly. Then near the end of the summer, we can announce our engagement. We don't have to get married, just be engaged for six months. Then after the appointments, we can quietly announce we will not be getting married."

Bailey chuckled lightly. "So if you get the appointment and we call off the engagement, won't that look suspicious?"

Xavier shook his head. "Yeah, you're probably right. So marry me, and we'll get a divorce in two years."

By the time they got inside her apartment, Bailey was thinking that this man was outside of his sane mind. "Alright, now, Mr. Monroe. You just sit down, and I'll make us some soup, sandwiches, and a nice cup of hot tea."

It took her only thirty minutes to get everything prepared. "Here we are," Bailey said, carrying a tray into the living room. "This is going to help you feel better."

She looked around. Xavier was not in the room.

Where is he? she thought. *I know he didn't leave.*

His coat, jacket, shirt, and slacks were thrown haphazardly over the back of the sofa, and his tie was on the table with his wallet, cell phone, watch, and cuff links. Bailey put the tray on the table and walked through her apartment.

Looking in the den, she saw he wasn't there, and there was no answer when she knocked on the door of the guest bathroom. Then, looking in her bedroom, she saw him there—sound asleep on her queen-sized bed, which seemed to dwarf him as he lay sprawled in the middle.

"Humph!" Bailey breathed as she hunched her shoulders, leaned over, pulled his shoes off, and draped the comforter over his long, muscular frame.

HOW

* * *

Early the next morning, Bailey heard her apartment door gently close. She sat up quickly and winced. Sleeping on the sofa in the den was definitely not as comfortable as her bed. As she was making her way to the bedroom, she noticed Xavier's clothes and belongings, which had been left in the living room, were gone. Entering her bedroom, she almost stumbled at the sight of her bed in total disarray.

She raised her hands to her hips. *He's gone, and he didn't even bother to strip the bed, much less attempt to make it up like it was before he passed out on it!* Laughing to herself, Bailey said, "You're giving him too much credit, Miss Thing. He's a man, and men don't think like that."

As much as she wanted to lie down and get back to sleep, she first stripped the bed, scented the mattress cover, took some fresh pillows from the closet, and scented the linens. Then she fell across the bed and slept for another couple of hours, finally getting the rest she desperately needed.

The day was going to be busy for Classic Party Planners. They had a senior citizen awards luncheon to serve in the early afternoon, and later that evening there was an anniversary reception to host.

Bailey managed to get through both occasions, but her mind kept wandering back to the events of the previous night. *Alcohol certainly makes fools of us all*, she thought. *I'll bet that man is somewhere right now trying desperately to remember what happened last night and asking himself how he ended up in my bed.*

Then, smiling to herself, she said, "I should have said yes to that silly proposal just to see his reaction."

Chapter 9: The Decision

Even though Bailey, Ja'Nell, and Bertha had serviced two events in one day, Bailey wasn't nearly as tired as she thought she would be. After the anniversary reception, she offered to buy the other two ladies dinner. Ja'Nell begged off because she had a date for brunch the next morning; Bertha offered her excuse, saying, "That sounds good, dear, but tomorrow is church, and I want to be rested for that. Will I see you there?"

"I'll be there," Bailey said.

When she got home, she climbed into bed, picked up the television remote, and settled in to watch whatever was playing on the Lifetime network. Halfway through a somewhat interesting drama, her phone rang, and she picked it up.

It was Xavier. "Good," he said, "you're finally home. I'm on my way over. I'll be there in twenty minutes, and I'm getting some Chinese food. Would you make some tea, please?" Then the phone went silent.

Bailey sighed, crawled out of bed, and changed into a pair of jeans and a T-shirt. Twenty minutes later, as she was brewing a pot of tea, the doorbell rang.

"Am I welcome in your home, Miss Anderson?" Xavier asked.

"I truly hope so, because I want to apologize for last night."

He looked so remorseful that Bailey couldn't help chuckling as she opened the door. "Don't just stand there, Mr. Monroe, come in."

With their plates full and their mugs brimming, the two sat at the kitchen table, each waiting for the other to initiate a conversation. Finally, Bailey asked, "How are you feeling?"

Xavier looked at her sheepishly. "Hung over. I was awake in your bed for an hour before I remembered where I was. By the way, your bed is very comfortable, and it smells wonderful. I think that's why I fell into such a deep sleep so fast. Now I understand why you're always in bed when I need to talk to you."

Bailey looked at him sternly. "The reason I'm in bed when you contact me is because you don't call at respectable times. I have a life away from Jackson and Monroe. I don't come home and sit around waiting with bated breath for your call."

After a quick laugh, he continued. "Anyway, I finally called my brother to come pick me up since he's the one that got me drunk in the first place. Much of my evening has evaded my memory. I hope I didn't say or do anything inappropriate. Will you forgive me for invading your home? I hope so. This dinner is a peace offering."

Bailey shook her head. "The only thing that happened was you fell asleep on my bed, forcing me to spend the night on the sofa in the den, and then you left my bed a disheveled mess with not so much as a goodbye."

Offering a remorseful look, Xavier said, "I'm sorry, Miss Anderson. Can you find it in your tender heart to forgive me?" He dropped his head and looked up at her through beautifully long, thick eyelashes, trying to look repentant. "Please? Pretty please? I promise that if I ever find myself drunk in your bed again, I will say goodbye before I leave your house in the morning."

They both laughed, but the jovial mood changed quickly when Xavier stood and stepped to her end of the table. He took her hands in his and knelt in front of her. "Don't think that I was too drunk to remember that I proposed to you."

Bailey tried to pull her hands away, but he held them tightly.

"No, please don't," he said. "I want you to know that I meant it. I want to ask you to do me that favor. Please, Miss Anderson. I will make it worth your while if you agree."

"You're really serious, aren't you, Mr. Monroe?" she asked, and he nodded his head. "I don't think we should do something like that. We're not that familiar with each other."

"I am serious. I really want to be in the district attorney's office, if not be appointed to be DA. It's been a dream of mine since I was twenty years old. And if not being married is the only thing holding me back, well… You don't have to answer me tonight, but please give it some consideration."

He patted her hands, stood, and took his place setting to the kitchen counter.

"Have a good night, Miss Anderson. I'll see you on Monday morning. Enjoy the rest of your weekend."

Bailey didn't attempt to show Xavier to the door. She remained seated at the table for an hour after his departure. She needed to think about his *proposal*.

A marriage of convenience. That didn't sound like an endurable union, but if that was all it would take to help him achieve his dream, who was she to stand in his way? Besides, what did she have to lose? She had no romantic entanglements. As a matter of fact, she had never had any romantic entanglements. And she wondered what it would be like to live with a man, even if it was only for a little while.

Well, in that case, she thought, *what's so bad about it? I probably have more to gain than I have to lose anyway.*

She smiled to herself, but as she cleaned the kitchen, took her shower, and prepared herself for bed, her mind kept wandering. She questioned herself, asking, *How could you consider something so preposterous? What will Mom say when she finds out about his proposal and his reason for proposing? How are you going to let him down?*

Getting through church service the next morning was difficult for Bailey, not only because she'd had a poor night's sleep but because she kept losing her focus. In her mind, she kept going over the situation, thinking of the pros and cons of a marriage of convenience.

How could you have been so thoughtless? How could you even consider marrying someone you don't even know outside of your work environment? she chastised herself.

She finally realized that if she was going to get some peace of mind, she had to talk to Xavier a little more to get a better understanding of what he expected of her during their two years of being "a happily married couple."

Getting to work Monday morning and finding out that Xavier wouldn't be in the office proved to make life even more stressful. She couldn't keep her mind on her work; she made mistakes she usually didn't make; she was uneasy and off balance. Everyone noticed she was not her usual everyday self, but they thought it best not to confront her. All except her mother.

On the way to the Classic Party Planners office on Tuesday morning, Bertha spoke up. "Bailey, what is wrong with you? You've been off balance for several days now. Do you want to talk about it?"

Bailey sighed. "Mom, you're right. Something is weighing on my mind, but I'm going to work it out before I talk about it."

She dropped her mother off at the office and continued on to her workplace down the street. When she stepped through the elevator doors onto the fifth floor, she almost collided with Xavier and Alexander Jackson.

"Oh, Miss Anderson! I'm glad you're here," Mr. Jackson said. "We are going to be out of town until Friday. Would you please take care of our calendars and appointments?"

She nodded her head. "Have a good trip. Don't forget to email me the details so I'll know how to reschedule your appointments."

As she started to walk away, Xavier touched her arm and then looked at his partner. "AJ, I need to say something to Miss Anderson. Why don't you go to the car? I'll be there is two minutes."

The elevator doors closed, leaving them alone in the hall.

Xavier said, "So, Miss Anderson, have you had enough time?"

"I would hate to stand between a man and his dreams," she said. "So yes, we can get engaged and then get married. Have a good day, Mr. Monroe."

She walked to her office without looking back.

You are such a wimp! she rebuked herself.

Chapter 10: Terms of the Contract

Friday was an easy work day, and because nothing urgent had been happening for several days, Bailey sent Ja'Nell home early. She locked the doors, put the phones on standby, and finished working on the contracts Mr. Anderson and Mr. Monroe had emailed her from Philadelphia. By the time she placed the last period on the last page, she was through for the day and left the office earlier than usual.

Because he had sent her a text message earlier in the day, Bailey knew Xavier was going to be at her apartment by 7 p.m. As promised, he showed up with a food offering. This time, it was two large pizzas and a six-pack of old-fashioned root beer.

The after-dinner conversation turned into a real business session. Xavier had drawn up a marriage contract that was very generous for Bailey. He cleared his throat, reached into his inside jacket pocket, and pulled out an officially certified marriage contract.

"Miss Anderson, I want you to know that I'm very serious about this arrangement and that I intend for it to be a marriage in the truest sense of the word," he told her. "That's why I want to review the terms of this contract with you so that there will be no misunderstanding later."

Xavier looked directly at Bailey, and when she made no comment, he opened the document and began detailing the terms of the agreement.

Bailey was in a flurry from the idea of it being a real marriage in "every sense of the word." After a few minutes, she broke the spell and regained her senses. She had to focus on the terms of the contract so that she could be sure she wasn't under any illusions when the contract came to an end.

According to the conditions of the arrangement, at the end of two years, there would be an amiable dissolution of the marriage, and Bailey Marie Anderson-Monroe would receive alimony for five years. She would be allowed to keep any possessions she had accrued during the marriage including all her personal items, clothing, and jewelry that had been acquired for or by her during the union. The final stipulation was that she had to surrender the right to continue the use of the Monroe name.

When Bailey appeared to be apprehensive, Xavier assured her she would not suffer financially or professionally at the termination of the marriage. With his best lawyer expression, Xavier said, "If you don't want to continue working for Jackson and Monroe, I'll help you grow your business into a full-time enterprise if you like. I'll do everything I can to ensure you don't suffer any setbacks because of the divorce."

Bailey looked directly at her boss and thought, *He truly wants this position.* At that moment, she felt a strong sense of compassion for him move slowly through her core.

With the contract signed, they settled down to making plans on how to go public with their engagement. "I think we should make an announcement in the newspaper and on certain social media sites," he said, being his usual levelheaded practical lawyer-minded self. "That makes it truly official and leaves no room for doubt."

Bailey remarked, "Don't you think that our parents should know before we inform the world? I'm sure my mother would certainly appreciate it."

"Well, how do you propose to break the news to them?" he asked.

"First, let's get our families together and make the announcement to them. Next, I think we should give ourselves at least a one- or two-month courting period so we can talk and get to know each other a little better. I don't know anything about you except your birthday is January 2nd and you hate surprise birthday parties."

Xavier chuckled and suggested that Sunday after church would be the perfect time for the two of them to go to their family members and make their announcements.

With that done, he stood and Bailey walked him to the door, offering him her hand. "Good night, Mr. Monroe."

Xavier took her hand and pulled her into a quick embrace. "I think we should be a little more amiable toward each other so that people will believe we're a real couple. Call me Xavier." He stepped back through the open door, still holding her hand. "Be ready by nine o'clock tomorrow morning. We have to get an engagement ring for you."

Bailey looked at her boss in wonder. "An engagement ring? You're going to invest in an engagement ring for me to wear? I thought we were going to date first."

Xavier offered Bailey a look of somber astonishment. "Yes, we are going to get an engagement ring. Being engaged is dating. I want people to believe that we are in love and that we want to be married."

Chapter 11: Engagement

The ring buying experience was a memorable one for Bailey. She got to see Xavier exhibit an air of deportment that was unfamiliar to her. When he picked her up in the morning, the first thing Bailey noticed was that Xavier was smiling. He spoke gently and was sociable, good-natured, and cheerful.

"Good morning, Bailey," he said. "Are you ready for this?" He held out his hand and guided her out of her apartment, took her keys, locked the door, and then put her keys in his pocket.

That was when she noticed the next thing about him. Xavier was wearing a corduroy jacket over a silk T-shirt that hugged the contours of his well-chiseled chest. It was neatly tucked into a pair of jeans that snugly fit his thighs. On his feet, he sported a pair of brown suede hush puppies.

"Stop looking at me like that," he told her. "Close your mouth. I do relax sometimes. I know how to be down, funky, and loose. I can get down with my bad self."

That was when Bailey lost control. She couldn't believe her ears. She started to laugh so hard that tears welled up in her eyes, and she nearly lost her balance. "Oh, you are definitely down. You may even be funky. But please, please don't ever say that again." She fell against him, and without thinking, he put his arms around her.

"Okay, that's enough, Miss Anderson," he said with a broad smile. "We have lots to do today. First, I want to dress up that ring finger of yours."

They untangled themselves and stepped into the elevator just as Ms. Fonteyn, Bailey's next-door neighbor, walked in behind them. "Good morning, little Miss Bailey, and who is this?" she asked. "Is this who that masculine voice that's been coming from your apartment lately belongs to?"

Embarrassed, Bailey smiled and nodded. For the duration of the elevator ride, the senior woman flirted with Xavier so much so that Bailey had no choice but to introduce them. Ms. Fonteyn took the opportunity to ask several personal questions. "Mr. Monroe, have you and Bailey known each other very long? Where did you two meet?"

Xavier offered Ms. Fonteyn a very cordial smile and sweetly answered her questions without any hesitation. He even looked at Bailey with soft, loving eyes. It was the icing on the cake when the elevator stopped and Xavier took Ms. Fonteyn's elbow, escorting her from the elevator and kissing her hand. "Madam," he said, "it has been a true pleasure to make your acquaintance. I hope that we meet again soon."

He offered Bailey his arm and as they headed for the outside door, Ms. Fonteyn pointed and called out to Bailey, "You done finally found yourself a winner, little girl. You better keep him!"

Xavier gave Bailey a sidelong glance. "Is there something I need to know about you and your love life? Do you have trouble keeping a boyfriend, Miss Anderson?"

Bailey returned the slanting gaze. "Mr. Monroe, until you share the details of your love life with me, I'm not telling you anything about my personal life."

Xavier offered her a half-smile and nodded. He took her elbow and said, "Soon enough, Miss Bailey, soon enough. Now here, let me help you into the car, your neighbor is watching us."

The couple arrived at The Jewelry Emporium in a jovial mood. As they entered, they were greeted by a man who appeared to be a slightly older version of Xavier. The man said, "X, come on in, man!"

As it turned out, the owner of the very beautiful, well-stocked jewelry store was Clayton Monroe, Xavier's older brother. He turned to Bailey, offered his hand, and without looking at his brother, asked, "So this is her?" Not waiting for an answer, Clayton gave Bailey's hand a light squeeze. "I'm glad to meet you, Miss Anderson. My little brother has been talking my ear off about you."

After the introductions, Clayton became all business. "Alright, young lady, since you are determined to make an honest man out of my baby brother, tell me. What type of ring would you like?"

Xavier spoke up. "Clay, like I said earlier, I want to get Bailey a ring that reflects her personality. Something bright, unique, and warm."

Two hours later as they were leaving the jewelry store, Bailey could not stop smiling. "This is the most beautiful ring I've ever seen. Do you really like it? Are you sure it's not too much? I can't believe it! This is a beautiful ring!"

She wore a medium-wide platinum band with two rows of channel-set diamonds on each side that cradled a 1.5-carat marquise white-light diamond set at an angle in the middle of the exclusive, one-of-a-kind setting.

Xavier took her hand and looked at the ring. "Yes, it is a beautiful piece of jewelry, and it does look good on your hand." He raised her hand to his lips and then looked into her eyes. "Thank you so very much, Miss Anderson, you don't know how much this means to me." Neither moved for a few seconds as they stood looking into each other's eyes.

"Umm… Oh…" Bailey stammered. "You are…you are quite…welcome."

Xavier released her hand, cleared his throat, and stepped back. "Are you hungry? Let's go get something to eat. Shopping makes me hungry."

He took her to a takeout restaurant well known for its grilled sandwiches. They engaged in small talk as they waited for their orders to be filled. Back in the car, Bailey had no idea where they were going. She didn't ask any questions, she just sat back and enjoyed the ride. After a few minutes, they arrived at Montclair Heights, the new subdivision in the upscale part of the city. It was all mini-yuppie mansions, condominiums, and townhouses, and they were well out of her range. Bailey had never been to this part of the city before.

"Why are we here?" she asked.

"I thought we could eat at my place. These sandwiches will be stone cold if we drive back to your apartment." He pulled the car into the driveway of a home with a well-manicured lawn and a multicolor tile-paved driveway that wound to the back of the house and ended at a four-car garage.

The inside of the stately home was spacious and well-planned. It appeared to have been professionally decorated and maintained. It was beautiful, but cold and impersonal. Everything was in its place, and there was no sign of dust anywhere. To Bailey, it didn't look lived in; it looked like a showplace. There were no delicate touches or dainty items anywhere, not even one knick-knack or framed family photograph.

She thought to herself, *This house is just like him—cold and unfriendly. What have I gotten myself into?*

Xavier was staring at her as if expecting her to say something. "This is a very nice house," she said. "How long have you lived here?"

"Thank you. I've lived here for three years. Would you like a tour?"

The rest of the dwelling was much the same as the entryway and the living room area: extremely neat and impersonal.

"Miss Anderson, do you like it? Do you think you could live here for two years?" Xavier asked.

He was so pleased with himself that she couldn't burst his bubble. "Yes, I love it. It's unbelievable. Yes, I could live here. Can I make some changes?"

Now it was his turn to laugh. "You sound just like my mother. She's always asking if she can add to the decor. She thinks it's cold and impersonal in here. Yes, you can change it, as long as you don't want to knock down any walls or add any new rooms."

They both laughed. Then they went into the kitchen where they talked while eating their sandwiches.

Chapter 12: Telling the Family

The following Sunday morning came quickly, and Bailey had to find something special to wear to church. Xavier was going to pick her up and take her to her family church so they could tell her mother the news. Then they would go to his parents' house for dinner and tell his family the news.

Bertha Anderson was surprised to see Bailey and her boss, Xavier Monroe, walk into the Greater Metropolitan Community Church together. She was even more surprised to have them walk up and sit in the same pew as her. Bertha was determined not to cause a scene, especially when these two had unintentionally done just that. She gave them both a motherly smile, shook hands with Xavier, kissed her daughter on the cheek, and hoped that the murmurings, elbow hunching, and wide-eyed stares would stop before the pastor got up to deliver the word.

The service proceeded and the final amens were pronounced. Then Xavier asked his mother if they could talk. She had already realized this wasn't just a random church visitation and was interested in hearing what the young man had to say. As they left the sanctuary, everyone was greeted by Pastor Jones, who raised his eyebrows when Bailey introduced Xavier to him. As far as the pastor could remember, Bailey had never been escorted to church by a man.

When the two men shook hands, Pastor Jones looked at Xavier very soberly and said, "We have a standing rule here at GMCC, Mr. Monroe, and that is that our young ladies don't kiss their boyfriends until I've met them. So since this is my first time meeting you, I'm sure you two will be kissing for the first time today." Releasing Xavier's hand, he turned to Bailey, winked, and kissed her cheek. "Hello, young lady, it's good to see you today."

Xavier was taken by surprise by the pastor's comment and didn't know how to respond. Bertha touched his arm. "Xavier, don't let this man rattle you, he's only joking." Then she turned to the pastor and said, "Marvin, you should be ashamed."

They all laughed. Everyone except Xavier.

After greeting Pastor Jones, the trio walked to the parking lot and stopped beside Bertha's car. "Mrs. Anderson," Xavier began, "I would like to ask for your permission to marry your daughter."

A few seconds passed, and she made no comment. She simply stood there looking at Xavier as if he were speaking a foreign language. Then, in a soft voice, she asked, "Is she pregnant?"

Bailey's eyes grew wide as she pulled in air. "Mom! Did you just ask that question, for real?"

After the initial shock, Xavier smiled broadly and shook his head. "No, ma'am. She's not pregnant. We are practicing celibacy until our wedding night. I want a wife, and your daughter has accepted my proposal. But I wanted to have your consent."

Hearing that, Bertha Anderson smiled and exclaimed, "Oh, my goodness! Oh, my goodness!" She started to cry, and Xavier gave her his handkerchief.

Some of the people stopped and looked. Pastor Jones quickly walked over to them. "Is everything alright over here? Sister

Bertha, are you okay?"

He looked from one to the other until finally, Xavier spoke up. "Pastor Jones, I just asked Mrs. Anderson for permission to marry her daughter. But she hasn't given me an answer yet."

The pastor smiled. "Well, don't just stand there, Sister Bertha, answer the young man."

Bertha reached into her purse and pulled out her fan. "I never thought I would hear anyone ask me that question. Yes, yes, yes! By all means, yes! You have my permission to marry my daughter." She grabbed them both in a hug and kissed Xavier on the cheek. Then she looked at Bailey and touched her cheek. "Congratulations, sweetheart. I hope that you both will be very happy for a very long time." She dabbed her eyes with the handkerchief. "Now let me see that ring that I've been puzzled about all morning."

It took another forty-five minutes for them to leave the church parking lot. Xavier had to be introduced to everyone, and everyone had to look at and comment about the ring.

As they drove to Xavier's parents' home, he said, "I never expected that to happen. Your mother was so happy. I wonder how my parents will react."

Bailey looked at him strangely. "What do you mean? Do you think there might be a problem?"

Xavier half-smiled. "No, I don't think there's going to be a problem. I think that my father is going to ask me if I'm sure this time."

"This time? Is there something you should tell me? Have you been married before?"

"No," he replied. "I was left at the altar ten years ago. It's a long story. We can talk about it one day." With that said, they arrived at the Monroe mansion.

Bailey sat in the car looking out the window. "This is a huge house. It's even bigger than yours. How long have your parents lived here?"

"This is my childhood home. It was a wedding gift to my parents from my great-grandfather Edgar Carter, my mother's grandfather. His father built it in the early 1900s when he moved here from Buxton. He was a coal miner who purchased several worked-out mines and later discovered that just a mile below the base level of the principal mine were several layers of diamond-producing rock. A couple of the other mines were found to have some rather large silver veins."

Bailey couldn't believe her ears. Xavier was a member of a family that had what some called "old money."

"That's interesting. So you and your brother had this big house as your playground. That should have been lots of fun."

"Clayton is not my only sibling. I have three brothers and two sisters. The oldest is Zane, he's a geologist. Next is Clayton, you know that he's a gemologist. Then Victor and Victoria, the twins. Victor is the head of cardiac surgery at Benton General, and Victoria Grace is the director of pediatric nursing at Benton General. The second sister is just before me, and her name is Olivia. She's a loan developer for home mortgages and small businesses, and her husband, Trevor, is an engineer."

A stately-looking older man dressed wearing white gloves and dressed in a suit with a short jacket opened the front doors. "Good afternoon, Mr. Monroe. Your parents are in the great room; I'll announce you."

"Good afternoon, Gregory," Xavier said. "Don't bother. I believe they are expecting me."

With a nod and a slight bow, Gregory closed and locked the house door, turned, and walked through a small arched doorway at the far end of the foyer.

Xavier took Bailey's elbow and led her toward an archway across the entry hall. As they descended four steps, Xavier said, "Mom. Dad. Hello." He shook hands with his father and kissed his mother on the cheek.

Judge Monroe looked at Bailey and nodded. "Now, son, what is the big deal? Why did you want to talk to us before the rest of the family got here?"

Xavier stepped close to Bailey and slid his arm protectively around her waist. "I've asked Miss Anderson to be my wife, and she has consented."

Helen was surprised, but she smiled cordially. The judge, however, immediately stepped forward and placed a hand on his son's shoulder. "Let's have a word, Xavier." He led Xavier a few steps away from the women and whispered, "Are you sure, son? Do you really want to try this again?"

Before Xavier could answer, Helen spoke up. "Be still, Melvin. Does he look like he's having second thoughts? Your behavior is causing concern for Miss Anderson." She turned to Bailey and offered her hand. When Bailey reached out, she found herself in an embrace. "Miss Anderson, congratulations, and welcome to the family."

When she stepped back, Helen asked if they had selected a wedding set yet.

This was the regularly scheduled Sunday that the Monroe siblings met to have their customary monthly family dinner. By the time the rest of the family members arrived, Helen was overly excited as she demanded, "Listen up, everyone, Xavier has an announcement to make."

Again, Xavier slid his arm protectively around Bailey's waist. "This lady is Miss Bailey Anderson, soon to be Mrs. Xavier Monroe."

The room seemed to explode with activity. Bailey was congratulated, hugged, picked up, swung around, and kissed on the cheeks. As a final point, Clayton said, "Show them the hardware, Bailey."

After the oohs and ahhs were over, the brothers and sisters and their spouses introduced themselves. Then Gregory announced, "Dinner is served."

During dinner, the brothers and sisters decided to give Xavier a hard time. They told stories about their bratty little brother and how much of a pest he had been to them. They talked about some of the little-boy things he'd done, like the time he climbed to the highest diving board at the country club pool and then was afraid to jump off, and how they'd played rock, paper, scissors to decide who was going to go up and get him.

Clayton held up his hand, laughing. "I lost, of course, so I had to go get him. It was hilarious. Bailey. X thought we were going back down the ladder. But I grabbed him and jumped. He screamed like a girl all the way down."

"And he has never let me fail at anything else in my life, either," Xavier said with a broad smile.

The brothers fist-bumped. Then Clayton proudly said, "That's what big brothers are for."

Chapter 13: Is This a Problem?

At the dinner table, the brothers and sisters continued with their stories. Olivia added information about how sweet Xavier could be, and she shared how he took care of her and her husband, Trevor, when her business was not yet well established and Trevor was laid off. With a tear in her eye, she told Bailey that it was her baby brother who paid their rent for a year and helped her husband get into the University of Iowa school of engineering.

"Olivia," Xavier said irritably, "do you always have to tell everything?"

Her immediate reply was, "No, not everything, my dear little brother; but I tell this story to show our sincere and never-ending appreciation for what you did for us."

After several more stories, Victoria asked, "Miss Anderson, has Xavier told you that he was left standing at the altar a few years ago?"

"She already knows, Vickie, let it go," Xavier insisted.

To lighten the mood, Clayton told everyone, "Xavier chose Bailey's ring." He relayed the whole story, adding that Xavier had wanted the ring to be a true symbol of Bailey's charms. Then he added, "Listen up, everyone, I don't know if he told anyone this, but he describes Miss Anderson as warm, unique, and bright."

Clayton's comment brought small laughs and quick side glances abounding around the table. For a few minutes, things settled down, and the focus was taken off Xavier.

"Miss Anderson, are you from Creston?" Victoria asked.

Xavier smiled and touched her shoulder. "That's Vickie-talk for 'hurry up and tell me your life story.' But you don't *have* to tell *her* anything, Bailey."

Bailey smiled and then shared that she and her mother had lived in Creston all of her life. But before she could offer any more information, she was interrupted.

Zane, Xavier's oldest brother, asked, "When did you ask her to marry you, baby brother? Was it the night you got drunk and 'fell asleep' at her apartment?" He smirked as he put his fingers in the air like quotation marks and let his voice drop when he caustically spoke those words.

There was a pause as the intended meaning of the question settled into everyone's minds. All of the brothers and sisters abruptly quieted down as each turned to look at Bailey.

"Zane," Olivia said, "why did you do that? You are such a jerk. Why can't you just be happy for our brother and Miss Anderson?"

Zane stood up and staggered slightly. "I'm just trying to see if it's love, lust, or gold-digging."

Xavier jumped up from his chair. "That's enough, Zane! I'm not going to let you ruin this for us."

Just as quickly, Clayton and Victor jumped up and grabbed their youngest brother's arms while the other family members all began to talk at the same time. During the commotion, no one noticed that Bailey had fled the room. But shortly, Xavier turned to the empty chair. Looking around, he asked, "Where is she?"

He pulled away from his brothers and ran from the dining room. In the foyer, Gregory pointed to the door of the guest bathroom. Xavier knocked once. "Bailey?"

She offered a soft "Yes?" and when he opened the door, she was standing by the vanity, looking into the mirror trying to repair her makeup. Bailey had two questions looping through her mind: *How did I let this happen? What have I gotten myself into?*

"I'm sorry," Xavier said slowly. "My brother is a drunken jerk."

A tear slid down her cheek. "Do you still want to do this? Is that what your family will think of me? They don't know me. They don't know that I'm not that kind of person."

She offered him the ring back. He took it but held onto her hand. "Come with me," he said, and when she hesitated, he put a hand on her shoulder. "Don't worry about Zane, just come with me and let me do the talking." When she tried to back away, he stepped closer to her and dropped his hand to the small of her back. "Come on, Miss Anderson. Trust me, please."

By the time they walked back into the dining room, things had quieted down. Xavier led Bailey back to her chair at the table. He stood behind her with his hands resting on her shoulders. "When I first asked Bailey to marry me," he said, "I had been drinking. She thought I was drunk and crazy, so she turned me down."

He looked at his oldest brother.

"I got drunk, Zane, trying to get up the nerve to ask her. And being the caring person that she is, she took me home with her so that I wouldn't be driving around under the influence. And yes, I fell asleep in her apartment while she was preparing a meal to sober me up."

Xavier looked around the table at his family members.

"I fell asleep on her bed. She threw a blanket over me and slept on the sofa in her den. Her compassionate, nonjudgmental attitude is part of why I love her so much."

Bailey stiffened, but Xavier squeezed her shoulders and continued.

"Then last week, I went to her again and told her that I want to be married and that I want her to be my wife. And now after your stupid statements, she just gave me the ring back. I need her to know that it doesn't matter to me what you think because this is my life, not yours. Furthermore, I'm not asking for, nor do I need, your approval to marry this woman."

Xavier stepped around the chair and knelt down to face Bailey

"Miss Bailey Anderson, I'm asking you again, in front of witnesses this time. Will you consent to becoming my wife?"

Victor cleared his throat. "Miss Anderson, I'll vouch for our little brother here. He's a first-rate guy, and we all have wanted to see him happily married for a few years now, so please, say yes."

Bailey looked at Xavier and heard him whisper, "Please?" Then he raised his hand slowly, resting the back of it on her hands in her lap, and opened his fingers. "Besides, we already have the ring."

He looked so sincere that Bailey couldn't resist. She nodded her head, gazed into Xavier's eyes, and said, "Mr. Monroe, I would be honored to become your wife."

Everyone around the table cheered and clapped except for Zane, who stood up forcefully, knocking his chair to the floor.

Xavier slid the ring back onto Bailey's finger, stood, helped her from the chair, and hugged her. The remaining members of the Monroe family were all pleased with Bailey's acceptance of Xavier's proposal despite the reaction of Zane, who stormed from the room in an alcohol-fueled huff.

Driven by his anger, Zane headed straight for the front door of his parents' house. Before Gregory could get there, Zane flung the door open. He stopped in his tracks when he heard the upsurge of cheerful sounds made by everyone.

He was so incensed that he could do nothing but stand on the front landing and breathe deeply, trying to calm himself down.

"I don't know who that trick thinks she is, but I'm not about to let her become part of our family and ruin my brother's life," he ranted to himself as he angrily stomped down the driveway, slid behind the wheel of his car, and drove away with screeching tires.

Chapter 14: Plans

The ride to Bailey's apartment later that night was a quiet one. Neither she nor Xavier spoke a single word. He escorted her to her apartment, opened the door, handed her the key, and left without comment. Later, the phone rang, and when Bailey answered, she heard Xavier softly ask, "Are you ready to go public with the engagement announcement?"

He waited patiently until she answered him just as delicately. "Yes, I'm ready."

Xavier returned with, "Alright, then, we'll make the announcement to our coworkers in the morning. Good night, Miss Anderson. And please be sure to wear your ring."

On Monday morning, Bailey arrived at the office at her usual time, 7:30 a.m. She was still confused about Zane Monroe's reaction to the announcement. She still had not received an explanation as to why it even happened.

Xavier had not yet come into the office, and she hoped he would show up soon. His tardiness caused her to worry; he was usually a very prompt person. If he didn't come in soon, she would have to tell her coworkers the news herself without him by her side and pretend to be happy about it. Again, she thought, *How did I let*

HOW

this happen? What have I gotten myself into?

After two hours, Bailey was having second thoughts about sharing the "good news" with her coworkers. She went back and forth in her mind contemplating whether to remove her ring or not. It wasn't until Ja'Nell was standing at Bailey's desk reviewing a document that the decision was made for her. The young receptionist picked up Bailey's hand and asked, "Miss Bailey, what is this?"

Forcing a smile to her lips, Bailey looked at the ring and then met Ja'Nell's eyes. "It's my engagement ring. I got engaged over the weekend."

With wide eyes, Ja'Nell made a gasping sound. "Engaged? To who?"

Bailey raised her hand to her chest and then warmly and tenderly replied, "Mr. Monroe proposed to me, and I accepted."

"What?" Ja'Nell asked, her voice full of surprise. "No! No way. You're lying. You're going to *marry*...the *Iceman*? When did this happen? You never said anything about going out with him. How come I didn't know anything about this?"

"Because who I have a relationship with is none of anybody's business until we get to the engagement stage, where I am right now," Bailey replied.

Throwing her arms around Bailey, Ja'Nell said, "Well, I guess you told me. Let me see that ring again, girl." Ja'Nell told the rest of the office, and one by one they came to say congratulations and to see the ring.

Xavier had a final sentencing hearing to attend first thing that morning, which was why he was late coming in. It took longer than expected because the judge wanted to interview several of the jury members. During that time, the courtroom was in lockdown and no one was allowed to leave or make any outside communications.

Of course, Xavier wasn't happy about the situation. He was

concerned that Bailey wouldn't be able to handle the cascade of attention their engagement announcement would bring, especially if there were any reactions along the lines of his brother's last night.

He thought, *What was that all about, anyway? Sometimes I can't believe him.* But he couldn't worry about that for long or he would lose his focus and his client could suffer a reversal of decision.

The moment Xavier arrived at the office, his partner, Alexander Jackson, called him into his office. "From what I've been hearing all morning," Jackson said, "it appears you're ready to try the marriage thing again. Is it true, are you?" Xavier nodded, and Jackson leaned forward and whispered, "Does she know about Priscilla Grayson?"

With a grin, Xavier leaned in and whispered, "Yes, a little. Not the whole story."

"Man, what are you waiting for?"

"I plan to take her to dinner tonight and tell her the whole story," Xavier said. "And why are we whispering?"

Jackson stood and stepped to his partner, extending his hand. "Well, then, congratulations, partner. I think Miss Bailey Anderson will make you a fine wife."

Xavier went looking for Bailey to invite her to dinner, but she wasn't at her desk. He found Ja'Nell sitting at the desk. "Where is she, Ja'Nell?" he snapped.

"Oh, Mr. Monroe. Miss Anderson…she…she went to lunch. She'll be back soon." As Xavier was walking away, Ja'Nell stood and thrust an envelope at him. "Mr. Monroe, this was delivered earlier today for you, and the lady said it was extremely important."

With a brief glance at the small personal-sized envelope, he slid it into his inside jacket pocket. Then he looked at the young receptionist and tersely declared, "Let me know the instant Miss Anderson returns from lunch."

Then he turned and treaded heavily to his office.

Later, when Bailey returned from lunch, Ja'Nell sat quickly upright. "Girl, Mr. Monroe is *on* one. He's waiting for you in his office. He said to let him know the instant you came in." When it buzzed, Ja'Nell pressed the intraoffice intercom button on her desk console and spoke through her headset. "Yes, Mr. Monroe. Sir. She's right... Yes, sir." She turned to Bailey. "Mr. Monroe is hot about something. You better get going."

Bailey smiled at Ja'Nell and went to the closet to hang her jacket. "Thanks for covering for me. I managed to help Mom with the registrations at the medical convention's opening reception. You can go home tonight. Everything is done. But don't forget that we're all working both Thursday and Friday evening."

When Ja'Nell made no comment, Bailey turned to see her staring at something across the room.

A gruff voice boomed, "Miss Anderson, I don't like to be kept waiting. This is a place of business, not a gathering place for a gossip session." Xavier turned and stomped back to his office.

Bailey looked at Ja'Nell and said, "Close your mouth. His bark is worse than his bite."

Ja'Nell shuddered. "Well, I guess I can take your word for it. I sure don't want him to bite me so's I can find out. You best get in there, Miss Bailey."

Bailey tapped lightly on Xavier's office door. "Come in," he barked gruffly.

"Was there something you needed, Mr. Monroe?" Bailey asked in a calm, professional voice as she stepped in and closed the door.

"My client is being released from state's custody today around five o'clock," he told her. "The district attorney's office discovered that at least two of the jurors had been approached during the trial, and that compromised the jury's ability to reach a true unbiased verdict. So tonight, my client is being turned over to the FBI to be placed in protective custody."

Bailey noted Xavier's face was set in a deep scowl; his forehead was furrowed, his eyes were coal black, and his jaw was clamped so tightly that she could see the muscle jumping.

"I wanted to talk to you about how it went today when everyone found out about the engagement," he continued. "And I also wanted to have dinner with you to discuss some other business, but I don't know how long this is going to take." He looked at her despondently. "And to top it off, when I finally made it back to the office, you weren't here, and I had to wait for over an hour before you got back to the office."

Xavier saw Bailey's sympathetic expression, and then he heard her tender voice say, "It will take as long as it needs to, Mr. Monroe. We can talk tomorrow. As for right now, you need to take care of your professional obligations because they always come first." She walked to his office door and, as it was closing, she said, "Have a good night, Xavier."

The rest of the week was busy. Bailey's evenings were occupied with Classic Party Planners hosting the medical convention and reception. On Friday night, Bailey was the social hour pre-banquet activities hostess. All of that meant Xavier and Bailey had to wait until the following weekend to get together.

Chapter 15: Family is Important

Bailey's doorbell rang that Saturday morning. She could tell by the way it chimed that it was not Xavier, her usual weekend visitor. She opened the door and was surprised to see her mother, Xavier's mother, and his two sisters, Victoria and Olivia.

"Ladies," she said. "Good morning. Please, come in."

Good thing I followed my mind and got up early. This could have been embarrassing, she thought as she opened the door wide.

Bertha Anderson stepped aside and ushered the ladies into her daughter's apartment. "We met in the elevator," she told Bailey. "Why didn't you tell me you were having guests this morning? I would have stayed home."

"Bertha, she didn't know we were coming," Helen said. "Now that I think about it, this is rather rude of us. We can come back if this is a bad time."

"No, no, please come in," Bailey insisted. "This is as good a time as any. Xavier has been showing up on Saturdays lately. He claims he's trying to get a look at his future. He alleges he needs to see what I look like on the weekends when I don't have to 'fix up' for work."

Making a tsking sound, Helen said, "Oh, my goodness. I don't know where we went wrong with that boy." Xavier's sisters looked at each other and chuckled.

Bailey ushered the four ladies into her living room. "Please, have a seat, ladies. I'm going to make some tea."

Before she could leave the room, Helen stepped to her. "Miss Anderson, this is not a formal visit. If it's all the same to you, can we sit in your kitchen?"

With that said, the ice seemed to have been broken, and a bond of friendship was forming. Bailey's kitchen was transformed into a sister-girl meeting place. The ladies talked while Bailey made cups of honey ginger tea.

Then Olivia suggested, "This tea is good, but since we are here at such an early hour, let's have breakfast."

Everyone agreed, and each lady took on a specific task. Bertha Anderson made a pan of delicious, flaky, buttery biscuits. Victoria cooked bacon and sausage. Olivia brewed coffee and prepared orange juice, while Helen Monroe made the cheddar cheese grits and fluffy scrambled eggs.

When the plates were all prepared and the five new friends were sitting around the kitchen table, the talk turned to the wedding. Questions were asked all around. Had a date been set? Had Bailey found her gown? What would be her colors?

Bailey held up her hands. "Hold it, ladies, we have only been engaged for three weeks. Xavier and I haven't even discussed these things ourselves."

"Girl," Olivia injected, "baby brother won't want to have anything to do with wedding plans. So, after the two of you have agreed on a date, we"—she pointed to each of the ladies at the table—"will be ready, willing, and able to help you organize and plan your special day."

They all nodded their heads in agreement. Just then, the doorbell began to ring insistently, accompanied by persistent knocking.

"Who is that?" Bertha asked, getting up.

"It's Xavier," Bailey said. "No, Mom, you all sit here. I'll get it."

When she opened the front door, Xavier said, "What took you so long, woman? Are you still in bed? Get up, half the morning is gone." He seemed to be in an especially good mood this morning.

Before Bailey could comment, a voice from the kitchen rang out. "Is this how you treat all women or just the one you've asked to marry you? I thought you were raised better than that."

Surprised, Xavier looked at Bailey, who hunched her shoulders and pointed him in the direction of the kitchen. "Mom?" he called out. "Is that you? What are you doing here?" As he stepped into the kitchen, he exclaimed, "Oh, wow! Mrs. Anderson. Mom. Olivia and Victoria! Man, don't tell me I've stepped into a hen party! I...I've got to go."

He briefly held Bailey's hand, turned on his heel, and stormed to the front door. "I'll be back later. Don't let them rattle you!"

The door clicked closed, and effervescent laughter mushroomed from the kitchen.

* * *

By seven o'clock that evening, Bailey had just about recovered from the surprise visit and was at her desk with her mother reviewing receipts from the week-long medical convention reception Classic Party Planners had hosted.

"I think we're going to have to hire another part-time worker, Mom," she said. "What do you think?"

Just as they began discussing their options, the doorbell rang.

"Mom, would you get that for me?" Bailey asked. "I'm going to close out the books, shut down this program, and I'll be right out."

When Bertha opened the door, Xavier was already speaking. "One minute, seventeen seconds. What took so long, Miss Anderson? Oh! *Mrs.* Anderson. Excuse me." He exhaled loudly. "Whew! I didn't know Bailey still had company."

Bertha just laughed. "You may want to work on how you greet my daughter, Mr. Monroe." She shook her head and held out her hand, inviting him into the apartment. "Tell Bailey I said goodnight, and I hope to see you two in church tomorrow. And remember: Be nice! You are not married yet!" She lifted her purse and jacket from the coat rack, stepped into the apartment hallway, and closed the door.

Xavier was still looking at the closed door when he heard a light ripple of laughter behind him. He turned to see Bailey. "Did I just give her reason to believe I would make a terrible son-in-law?" he asked.

Bailey laughingly told him that her mother probably would never think badly of him, "mainly because she's so happy I'm getting married, she would forgive you for almost anything." Then she added, "You know she never thought I would make her a mother-in-law."

When Xavier made no comment, Bailey looked at him and noticed that he looked stressed. His lips were pressed into a tight line, and his eyes were intense. The atmosphere in the apartment changed quickly; it became somber and reserved.

Lightly taking her by the elbow, Xavier guided Bailey into her living room and sat in the armchair across the room from her. "Bailey, we need to talk: You should know the whole story about my being left at the altar."

Bailey had no idea what to say, so she just sat on the couch looking at him. She had never before seen him so fallible.

Xavier rubbed his hands together and leaned forward. Then he linked his fingers together, rested his elbows on his knees, and let his linked hands hang. Staring at the floor, he began to talk.

"I had no idea that it was going to happen. Priscilla. Her name is Priscilla Grayson. My sister Victoria is married to her brother, Caleb. Priscilla and I had been friends from the time we were in elementary school. Our parents were best friends, and so we spent much of our lives in each other's company."

Slowly, Xavier leaned back into the chair, rested his head on the cushioned back, and rubbed his hands up and down his thighs. There was a sad smile on his face.

"We did almost everything together, and for a while, whenever you saw one of us, you saw both of us. Priscilla even became one of the guys." He gave a small laugh. "That is until she started to look less like a boy and more like a young lady. Then I had to protect her from the guys."

Bailey sat across the room from her fiancé, watching him tell his story with a small ache in her chest. He seemed to be experiencing emotional turmoil, and as much as she wanted to, there was nothing she could do to help alleviate his discontent.

"We had our first drinks together," Xavier said, "we had our first sexual experiences with one another, and we even went to college together. So it was a natural thing, to me, that when we married, it would be to each other."

He huffed and continued. "Just before I graduated law school, we got engaged. At the same time, Priscilla had gotten interested in modeling and clothes designing. She had done some small-scale modeling and designing off and on throughout college. She didn't tell me that she'd applied for and gotten accepted to the International Fashion Institute in France, or that she had taken the offer. I found out she was gone through Covington, her chauffeur.

"On our wedding day, instead of Priscilla walking down the aisle in a beautiful white dress and veil, Covington walked down that aisle as the wedding march began to play and handed me a note. I didn't know what to do. I walked out of that church went back to my apartment and didn't leave for three weeks."

Xavier looked over at Bailey and smiled dejectedly. "I would have stayed longer, but I ran out of food, coffee, toilet paper, bath soap, laundry detergent, and paper towels." He stood and paced the small room, then reached into his inside jacket pocket and pulled out several small envelopes. "This is the note I got that afternoon at the altar." He held one tattered envelope up in the air, and then in his other hand, he held up several more. "And these have been sent to me within the last two to three months."

He sat on the couch next to Bailey.

"She's coming back, and she wants us to meet. She wants to know if there's a chance that we can reestablish our relationship."

Bailey opened her mouth to speak, but nothing came out. She stood quickly and walked to the window seat. "So," she eventually managed through a dry throat, "what are you going to do?"

Xavier moved across the room and stood before Bailey as she lowered her head, closed her eyes, and clasped her hands together in her lap. He leaned forward and covered her hands with one of his, squeezing lightly. "I want us to get married as soon as possible," was his reply.

She couldn't believe what she just heard. Was he serious? She lifted her head and looked into his eyes. "What?"

He sat down next to her. "I said I think that we should get married as soon as we possibly can."

Chapter 16: Rushed Plans

When Xavier and Bailey walked into the Greater Metropolitan Community Church and sat beside Bertha Anderson, it caused another commotion. This time, however, it calmed down quickly. For the couple, it seemed Pastor Jones was rather long-winded this morning. They were both apprehensive. Bailey fidgeted with her purse for most of the service, and Xavier squirmed so much that Bertha wondered if his pants had lost their crease.

When the service ended, Xavier touched Bertha's arm. "Ms. Bertha, would you have lunch with us this afternoon?"

"Why? What's wrong? What's going on?" Bertha looked from one to the other. "You two have been as restless and uneasy as a long-tail cat in a roomful of rocking chairs."

Bailey gave her mother a weak smile. "Mom, we want the families to spend some time together, that's all."

Everyone met at Xavier's house. The couple decided to tell everyone at the same time that they were planning on getting married by the third week of September.

Judge Monroe asked, "Son, what's the rush? Is something wrong?"

At that point, everyone began asking questions. Holding up his hand, Xavier said, "Listen, everybody, there is nothing wrong. We simply decided that we don't want a big wedding. We think, with all that's going on with my application for the position as the state's top attorney, that it's best if we have a small family gathering and then have a reception when we return from the honeymoon."

Bailey added, "It would be more meaningful to us if we have a small wedding with a few friends and loved ones. Would you support us on this, please?"

Bertha Anderson said to her daughter, "You know, Bailey, I'm going to support you in this decision, but I want you to know that I was dreaming of seeing you walk down the aisle in a beautiful white dress with a church full of people smiling and clapping."

"Mom," Bailey said, "I'm still getting married in church, and I'll definitely be wearing a beautiful white dress. We just won't be saying our vows to a capacity crowd." She assured her mother that the Anderson-Monroe wedding would be intimate as well as memorable.

Victor, who had been sitting quietly on the sofa, stood and sauntered up to his taller, more muscular younger brother. Leaning forward, he put his hand on Xavier's shoulder, and in a stage whisper, he said, "Let me have a quick minute with you, baby brother."

"What do you want, Vic? This is not the time for any of your shenanigans! Man, go back over there and sit down," Xavier said, pointing to the sofa.

But Victor was not put off by his younger brother's chastisement. In a significantly louder voice, he said, "Xavier, man, you getting married is something I've always hoped for you. But I never thought it would materialize, especially after what happened with Priscilla. After that, you vowed to be single for life, becoming, let's say, a prolific ladies' man. And now here you are, not only getting married, but you want to do a rush job on it? What's up, man?"

Xavier took a deep breath, and when he spoke, his voice carried a note of constraint. "Is it so beyond your thinking capacity to believe that I finally found a wonderful woman I want to spend the rest of my life with?"

Looking at his younger brother, Victor's smile broadened. "I don't doubt that Bailey is a wonderful woman, but does she know about some of your other women? Does she know that you are the consummate love-them-and-leave-them ladies' man?"

Bailey felt Xavier's body stiffen as he took her hand and held it with enough pressure to make it uncomfortable. From that small movement, she knew he was about to lose control of his temper. She quickly returned the pressure on his hand and felt him loosen his grip. Then she stepped closer to him and, as he turned to look down at her, she shook her head slowly with a half-smile. That was just what he needed to regain some semblance of self-control.

Choosing not to take in his brother's signs of discontent, Victor pressed forward with his commentary. "What you two are saying sounds legitimate, and if I weren't your big brother and didn't know you like I do, I wouldn't be feeling like there's something else going on here. So let's cut to the chase, Xavier. You might be fooling everybody else, but you are most definitely not pulling a fast one on me." He jabbed his index finger into Xavier's chest. "Now, how 'bout you tell us the real reason you two want to tie the knot so quickly?"

Xavier glared at his brother's lecherous smile. Then he dropped Bailey's hand and grabbed Victor's. A slow smile spread across Xavier's face.

Surprised by the intensity of Xavier's hold on him, Victor tried to pull his hand away, but Xavier increased the pressure. Victor winced in pain. The room grew ominously quiet. Everyone stood motionless, looking from one brother to the other.

Moving quickly across the room, Clayton, ever the peacemaker, calmly touched Xavier's shoulder. When he felt his younger brother's body relax, he said, "Let him go, X. Don't let him get to you like that." Then, to Victor, he said, "Shut up. Go sit down somewhere and leave them alone before Xavier whips your tail again like he did the last time you challenged his decision-making."

Xavier dropped Victor's hand, took hold of Bailey's shoulders, pulled her flush to his body, and pressed his lips against hers. After nearly thirty seconds, he finally broke the contact and rolled Bailey behind his back. Then, with a broad smile, he leaned into Victor's space and said, "Because we can't wait any longer. That's why. Now...*get out of my face!*"

Bailey gasped and hid her face in her hands as Xavier pulled her to his chest. With that, everyone in the room exploded into laughter and the brothers fist-bumped.

"That's more like it," Victor said. "*Now* you sound like my little brother. You should have known that you can't pull the wool over my eyes."

True to their promise, the women in the newly formed sister-girl club went into action. They had only six weeks to pull everything together. So it was that within three weeks, the ladies had helped the bride select a beautiful dress. And because Xavier's sisters were serving as her bridal party, they quickly selected their dresses, too.

The flower arrangements were donated by a member of the church who had watched Bailey "grow up into a wonderful young woman" and wanted to do something special for her. The job of decorating the church was to be done by the mothers.

Two weeks before the wedding, things had become stressful. The bride and groom only saw each other at work, and that was just in passing. Wednesday of that week found Bailey so tired that she couldn't wait to go home and get into her flannel pajamas. But before she could do that, she had errands to run. Who would have thought that shopping could be so strenuous? So many things to do and to buy just to get married. Bailey shook her head.

She didn't know what she would have done without her bridal checklist. Tonight, she was going for the final fitting of the gown. Then she had to make a spa appointment (firmly insisted on by her future mother-in-law), and finally, the hair appointment.

Just as she was putting the phones on stand-by and shutting down the computers, the doors to the office were snatched open. When Bailey turned around, she was looking at the mothers and the sisters.

"Oh, you guys, why are you all here?"

"We're here to ensure that all of the last-minute items on your bride-to-be checklist get done, so hand it over," Victoria said. She looked at the list. "Ladies, our first stop is Madam Ella's Bridal Gowns and Accessories. Then we're off to The Lingerie Shop." She pointed to Bailey. "You, young lady, need to get a bridal trousseau. Finally, we'll be going to Saks to find you a getaway outfit."

"Victoria, sis," Bailey said, "that's a lot to do in one night. I'm tired."

Olivia put a hand on her shoulder. "You don't have time to be tired, girl, you are getting married in two weeks. Besides, if you get everything done this week, you have next week to rest and get rid of those bags under your eyes. It's a good thing Momma went ahead and set that spa appointment for next Thursday. You really need the full treatment: manicure, pedicure, massage, and facial. Girl, you look wrung out."

"Baby," Bertha said, "have you and your man gone to get that license yet? Time is getting short, and all of this will be for nothing if you wait too long."

"We got our physicals and applied for and picked up the license the week we announced our final wedding plans at his house," Bailey informed her.

Satisfied, Bertha said, "Well, then, let's go. The sooner we get started, the sooner you can get home and get some sleep."

With a shake of her head and a smile on her tired face, Bailey led the ladies out of the office. Much later, she practically fell off the elevator on the fifth floor of her apartment building. She was tired but, thanks to the mothers-and-sisters crew, the last-minute items and final shopping had been accomplished. Despite being tired to the bone, she was very happy to have those things done.

Now, she thought, *the last thing for me to do at the office is to be sure that Ja'Nell is set up to take over while I'm away, and then all my worries should be over.*

She opened her apartment door to find the telephone ringing. She answered, and the voice coming through the receiver declared, "If you are not in the bed when I need to speak to you, then you are out in the street. Where have you been, Miss Anderson? I've been calling you for two hours."

"Mr. Monroe, I…" Bailey huffed. "Xavier, what can I do for you at ten o'clock at night? Why aren't you asleep?"

"I wanted to remind you that we have a counseling session in the morning with Pastor Jones and tell you that afterward, we will be going to lunch. I also wanted to tell you that I will be there to pick you up at 8:30 sharp. So be ready. Good night."

And just like that, the connection was broken. Bailey stood holding the receiver for a few seconds.

Why should I be surprised by his rudeness? she asked herself then put the phone on its base and went to her bedroom.

Chapter 17: Second Thoughts?

Bailey's doorbell chimed. "Who is it?" she asked in a sing-song voice, but she already knew who it was. She also knew that Xavier would be early, that he was hoping to find her still undressed, and that he was doing it just so he could have a reason to be cranky. He was in for a big disappointment

"Just open the door…please," came his terse reply.

Bailey grabbed her coat and purse, opened the door, and stepped into the hall. She locked her apartment door and walked down the hall toward the elevator. All the while, Xavier stood watching her.

"Well don't just stand there, let's go," she called over her shoulder.

Following her down the hall to stand beside the elevator, Xavier looked intently at his fiancée. "Why are you in such a hurry? We're going to be too early."

"You called me at ten o'clock last night and demanded that I be ready when you arrived. Well, I'm ready, so what's the problem?"

He looked at her with a half-smile on his face. "You are a very perplexing, young lady, Miss Anderson."

Bailey looked at him and stuck out her tongue. Now with a full smile on his face, Xavier cleared his throat and lightly touched her on the shoulder.

"Before we get on with our business, I have some good news and some bad news. Which would you like to hear first?" Xavier quietly and falteringly inquired of his future temporary wife.

With an uncertain expression and raised eyebrows, Bailey gave him a sidelong glance. "All of it," she said.

Hesitantly, he let his hand slide down her arm to gently capture her hand. "I'm leaving town tomorrow night. Beginning Monday morning, I start the final stage of official interviews before the final appointments for state attorneys are made. I'm going to meet with a coach this weekend. The interviews are a three-day process, and the finalist announcements will be made on Thursday."

Without thinking, Bailey quickly leaned forward and hugged Xavier. "Congratulations," she said. "God's blessings. I know that you will be very impressive. I'm so proud of you."

Realizing what she had done, she quickly attempted to release him from her hug, but Xavier smoothly wrapped her in his embrace. With one hand, he tilted her chin, lowered his head, and whispered, "Thank you."

Before Bailey could react, their lips touched. She was surprised but didn't hold back. She returned the kiss. Just as it was beginning to become more intense, the doors of the elevator opened and someone said, "Well, it's good to know that this is a healthy relationship."

Each quickly released their hold on the other and stepped back. Ms. Fonteyn was beaming at the couple as she stepped out of the elevator.

"You don't have to be ashamed. I think that young love is beautiful. By the way, I received my invitation, and I do plan to be there."

Embarrassed, the couple nodded their heads and then entered the elevator. Just before the elevator doors closed, Ms. Fonteyn smiled at Xavier and said, "That's a nice shade of lipstick, Mr. Monroe."

Bailey quickly handed him a tissue as they descended to the first floor in silence.

* * *

In Pastor Jones' study, they were instructed on the meaning and purpose of marriage; they were lectured on the importance of intimacy in the relationship and the need to love, honor, and respect themselves, their spouse, and the institution of marriage.

For Bailey and Xavier, the five hours spent in the pastor's study were challenging. It was a time of emotional highs and lows. The twosome was seated together on a loveseat as they were questioned, instructed, warned, admonished, and even congratulated for stepping into the confines of marriage.

At times, it was comforting to be sitting so close. At other times, it was uncomfortable, awkward, and even embarrassing. But they managed to make it through the session without letting the pastor know the real underlying reason for their marriage. After the counseling session ended, both were feeling like survivors of an intense interrogation.

Because of their emotional state, they decided not to go to lunch. Instead, they sat wordlessly in Xavier's car outside Bailey's apartment building, each caught up in their own thoughts while pretending to be looking at the activity going on around them.

"Bailey," he said, looking at her intently, "are you having second thoughts? If so, please don't let me wait to find out at the altar. I don't want to go through that again."

She returned his gaze and could tell that even though he was trying to lighten the moment, he was a little anxious. "Xavier, I made you a promise, and I intend to keep it," she assured him.

They looked at each other for a few moments. He reached over and took her soft, feminine hands into his masculine grip. Kissing the back of each hand, he whispered, "I appreciate that."

Bailey cupped his face in her hands. She looked pensively into his eyes and then leaned forward and kissed him gently on the lips. "Have a good trip. Do well in your interviews. I'll be praying for you. And don't you dare think about leaving me standing at the altar," she said, making her own feeble attempt at humor as he smiled weakly, nodded his head, and softly replied, "I won't. I promise."

Bailey quickly exited the car and walked hurriedly toward the building's entrance. Stepping briskly and refusing to look back, she made her way to the lobby. As soon as she stepped into the vestibule, she lost the battle with herself.

She looked back and saw Xavier standing outside of the driver's side of the car, looking at her. When she turned, he raised his hand slowly in a goodbye gesture. When she saw him raise his hand, she raised her own and pressed it against the cold glass door.

Xavier got back into his car, and Bailey turned away, struggling to hold back the tears. *If I can just make it to my apartment, I'll be okay,* she thought. She had to repeat it over and over to hold the full barrage of tears at bay.

Alone in her apartment, sitting in the window seat while time passed and the light of day slowly faded, Bailey thought back on what Pastor Jones had said about marriage being a union ordained by God between a man and a woman, and once married that a couple is joined for life in a special spiritual and physical relationship that is to be nurtured and cultivated sincerely and reverently.

What am I going to do? she asked herself. *I'm not the wifely type. I don't know how to be married. But I don't want to disappoint Xavier.*

She was feeling so down that she almost missed the buzz of her intercom. Slowly walking across her apartment, she reluctantly pressed the talk button. "Yes?"

The voice on the other end was upbeat and full of joy. "Bailey, it's us, Olivia and Victoria! Send the elevator down."

Bailey met them at the elevator, and when the doors opened, she saw the sisters weighed down with bags of food and their overnight cases. "Xavier said you might need some company tonight, so here we are."

It seemed that that gesture was the undoing of Bailey's resolve. Her tears began to fall again. Holding tightly to one another, the three women walked to apartment 502. Once inside, as they were unloading their arms Olivia asked, "Girl, what is going on? Why are you crying?"

"Okay, tell us," Victoria added, "what did baby brother do?"

When Bailey finally regained her composure, she explained it to the sisters. "Xavier and I just completed the pre-marriage counseling with the pastor, and it was a heavy session. And he's leaving town…and won't be back until just before the wedding…and I'm worried about whether he'll get the appointment or not, and…" Before she could say any more, fresh tears began to flow.

Victoria and Olivia looked at each other and said, "The jitters."

Olivia continued, "Sister-in-law, you have the before-the-wedding jitters. Don't worry, it's going to be alright."

"That's for sure," Victoria added. "It's clear that right about now, you need to have yourself some downtime."

The rest of the evening was spent in friendly companionship. The sisters prepared the food that they'd brought, and as the night progressed, the trio ate, drank wine, and had lots of girl talk. At around midnight, Bailey had to admit that she was in a more jovial mood than earlier in the evening. She hadn't laughed so much in her life. She was going to enjoy having these ladies in her life…at least for the next two years, anyway.

Finally, they all decided it was time to get some rest, so they climbed into Bailey's bed, put on a movie, and promptly fell asleep.

Chapter 18: That's Strange

The ringing of the alarm clock cut through Bailey's head like a knife. She was the first to awaken, but because of the hangover, she could hardly lift her head from her pillow.

"What is that noise?"

"Turn that thing off!"

"Oh, my goodness, why is it so loud?"

It seemed that the sisters were hungover too.

Bailey managed to roll over and hit the off button. Then she scooted out of bed and did a slow shuffle to the bathroom. In the midst of brushing her teeth, she remembered she had taken the day off, so she washed her face, combed her hair, and went to the kitchen to put on some water for tea.

By the time the water was ready, the sisters were slowly walking into the kitchen. "Girl," Victoria said, "you're going to be late for work. You better get going."

Handing each sister a cup, Bailey replied, "I took the day off to take care of the last-minute preparations, but since we took care of them on Wednesday, I have nothing much to do today."

"Ooh, what is this?" Olivia said, taking a sip from her cup. "It's delicious. I can taste ginger, orange, lemon, and honey."

"It's ginger tea," Bailey said. "It's supposed to help with hangovers."

For the next few minutes, the three friends sat in silence, drinking their tea. Finally, Victoria asked, "What are you going to do with your day?"

"Nothing, except maybe get a head start on my packing. But I'm going to do very little of that. Then, at five o'clock, Classic Party Planners has a reception at the Plaza. I'm the hostess, so let's have another cup of tea and get rid of this hangover."

* * *

The reception was the last soiree that Bailey would be putting on until after the wedding. She wore a purple cocktail dress with a black sweater jacket, and she wore her hair down, something she almost never did because it was so thick and wavy that it sometimes got out of control.

Tonight, however, she felt relaxed, lighthearted, and carefree. She thought about the fact that in eight days, she was going to be Mrs. Xavier Monroe, and for the next two years she was going to be one of the ones attending the party rather than being the one organizing and working it.

"Miss Bailey, girl, you look beautiful!" Ja'Nell was saying. "I'm glad you suggested purple and black as the theme colors. They look good together. Now let me take your picture for the photo disc before we get too involved in the business at hand."

After taking each other's pictures, the women went to work to make the reception a success.

HOW

* * *

Walking into her apartment at two o'clock in the morning was a relief for Bailey. The reception had been a triumphant success. She'd received requests from several guests for her business card so that Classic Party Planners could help them with their own receptions, cocktail parties, and fundraisers. It seemed the small business was making a name for itself, and this made Bailey very happy.

Only one thing had given her pause. She had been delighted to see her future in-laws in attendance, including Xavier's sisters. As they were talking, Victoria suddenly excused herself from the group and walked over to a tall, shapely, stunning woman. The two spoke for a short time. All the while, the beautiful woman gave Bailey several hard, prickly stares. Then she quickly left. Bailey thought it was strange but didn't have time to ponder it; she had a job to do. Thinking about it now, she shook her head, exhaled, and dismissed it.

By eight o'clock the next morning, she was up and out of her apartment. She was jogging around the fountain at Norton Hills Park, thinking about Xavier, praying that he would be successful next week and that he would get back to town in time for the wedding with a new title.

Lost in thought, she lost her footing when someone suddenly stepped onto the path before her, and she fell down. Holding her throbbing ankle, Bailey took a quick look at the retreating feminine figure, thinking that she looked like the woman from the reception last night.

As she slowly raised herself to her feet, Bailey once again looked back over her shoulder. The woman, whoever she was, was running away.

Chapter 19: The Storm Before the Calm

Getting through the weekend took some concentration for Bailey. She spent the rest of Saturday recovering from her jog. Even though she had twisted her ankle, it appeared that the support in her shoes had prevented any major injury from happening. After lightly wrapping her ankle, she turned her attention to getting rid of things she didn't want to put into storage or take with her to Xavier's house.

She hadn't gone for a run in about six months and felt stiff and fatigued, but she managed to get through her tasks before going to bed. Sunday was tough; for the first time in a while, Bailey went to church and had dinner alone.

Monday morning went as usual...until Bailey received a call from Xavier's brother Zane asking her to meet him for dinner. Though she was surprised as well as curious, she thanked him for the invitation and told him she had to turn him down because her schedule was full for the rest of the week.

At exactly 4:30 p.m., the Monroe sisters walked into the Jackson and Monroe offices, shoulder to shoulder. Bailey looked at her future sisters-in-law and asked, "Ladies, what are you doing here? Didn't we say we were going to meet at my apartment?"

"Yes, we know," Victoria said, "but we were downtown getting our last-minute shopping done and thought we could all have a little snack before you work us all night long."

Smiling, Bailey asked the ladies to wait while she finished showing Ja'Nell how to switch the phones to stand-by, check the associates' offices, and secure the administrative center before signing out for the day—after all, it would be Ja'Nell's job starting tomorrow until Bailey and Xavier returned from their honeymoon.

When the three finally walked into Bailey's fifth-floor apartment, she announced, "Let's start with the kitchen. Everything else is pretty much under control. The movers specifically asked me to separate and identify the things going to storage and the items going to Xavier's house."

The sisters looked at each other and laughed. "Girl, you are so silly. It's not just Xavier's house anymore, it's your house too," Olivia said.

"Yes, and I hope you can turn that mausoleum into a home," Victoria added joyously, "because right now, it's just a great big, cold, empty house."

Two hours into the final packing process, Bailey answered the insistent knocking on her apartment door. Zane was standing on the other side, wearing a sinister smile. In his hand was a bottle of white zinfandel.

"Hey," he said, "since we couldn't meet somewhere, I thought I could come here." He held up the bottle. "I brought some wine." He raised his eyebrows. "I think we should have a talk and get to *know* each other a little better."

Bailey invited him in. Zane stood in the living room and looked around the apartment at all of the boxes. "So, are you all ready for the upcoming nuptials?"

"Yes," Bailey said, "things are progressing very well, thank you."

The sisters recognized their brother's voice and Olivia started toward the kitchen door, but Victoria touched her arm, shook her head, and lifted her finger to her lips.

"Why are you trying to ruin my brother's life?" Zane threw out without warning. "You are nowhere near his type." He continued his oral assault, angrily declaring, "You may have my little brother fooled, but not me. I see you for what you really are, one of those gold diggers from the wrong side of the tracks who thinks she's latched onto a meal ticket. Let me tell you, you're just another one of those bedroom partners he's picked up, and he probably won't even show up for the wedding. He's going to leave you standing at the altar, so you should probably not even bother to show up yourself."

Bailey was taken aback. When she made no comment, Zane continued with great ferocity.

"What's the big hurry in getting married, anyway? I suppose you told him you're pregnant and he's trying to do the noble thing and protect your reputation. Is that it? Well, let me tell you, you're not going to get away with this charade, little miss trailer trash!"

Without a word, Bailey walked around Zane and opened her apartment door. "Now that you've had your say," she told him, "you need to leave my apartment, Mr. Monroe."

Zane quickly closed the space between them and grabbed Bailey's arm. "I'm not finished with you yet…"

Trying to pull away, Bailey declared, "You have no right touching me. You're hurting me. Let me go!"

At that moment, the Monroe sisters stepped out of the kitchen. "Zane!" Victoria exclaimed. "Get your hands off her! Are you out of your mind? Now I know that you heard Bailey ask you to leave, so get out!"

Quickly dropping Bailey's arm, Zane spun around. "Vicky, what are you doing here?" Then he looked past Victoria. "Livvie, you're here too?" He took a few staggering steps toward his sisters. "She's no good for our little brother, y'all know that. She's one of those gold diggers trying to use a strong successful man to get herself out of the ghetto."

Zane whirled around and raised his hand to Bailey, but before he could hit her, she touched his midsection with the stun gun she'd snatched from the table behind the door. Then, as he was falling, the sisters shoved Zane out the door, slammed, and locked it.

Olivia and Victoria turned and looked at Bailey. "Are you alright?" Victoria asked. "Did he hurt you?"

The three ladies stood in a tight embrace for several minutes until Olivia turned away from them, secured the chain, and cracked the door open to look into the hall. "He's gone," she announced. Then she put her arms around Bailey's shoulders. "Don't worry, girl. He's drunk, and I'm sure he won't be coming back here anytime soon."

They walked Bailey to the kitchen and sat at the table. "I want to apologize for our brother," Olivia said. "He had no right to say those things to you. Please know that the rest of the family doesn't feel like that. We're so glad that you and our little brother have found each other."

"We need to tell somebody what just happened," Victoria said. "I'm going to call Momma and Daddy."

"No," Bailey protested, "don't say anything to your parents. They might want to contact Xavier, and he doesn't need any more stress right now. Let's just finish packing up this kitchen and then we'll relax and have a glass of wine on big brother Zane." She smiled wanly. "He left a bottle of white zinfandel on the living room table."

It wasn't until 11:30 that night, after the ladies had gone and after Bailey had showered and crawled into bed, that she allowed the hurt and hatefulness of Zane's words to sink in. She cried herself to sleep. Her last thought before drifting off was, *How could our getting married cause others to be so hateful and aggressive?*

Chapter 20: Get Moving

Tuesday morning dawned, and Bailey was walking through her apartment checking and rechecking the multitude of boxes stacked throughout the rooms. "I can't believe how much stuff I had in this little place," she said to herself. Then she smiled and added, "After this marriage contract ends, I'll be sure to get a bigger place so that all of the stuff I'm keeping can fit."

The first truck to arrive was the Salvation Army, and they quickly collected the twenty-five boxes of clothing and small household items she was donating. Two hours later, the movers arrived. As they reviewed the plans, Bailey started to feel excited. The first stop was the storage unit; the final stop was at her mother's house, where her remaining clothes and other personal items were going to be stored in the garage and her old bedroom.

After things settled down and everything was in its place, Bailey sat with her mother for a cup of tea. "Mom," she said, "you haven't changed my old room at all. It still has the same curtains, comforter, and rugs. Why haven't you converted it into a sitting room or something?"

Bertha smiled wisely and replied, "I don't go in there much, maybe once a month to dust. I thought you would be back home one day, and this is my way of making sure that you would feel welcome." Mother and daughter laughed together. "So, dear, have you heard from Xavier?" she asked.

Bailey sadly answered, "No, not in the last couple of days. But the last time we did talk, he promised me that he would be back in town by Friday night."

For the rest of the afternoon, mother and daughter made small talk. After dinner, Bertha asked, "Do you have anything that you want to ask me? You know, about being married, or maybe even about the honeymoon? I mean, it's not too late to talk a little more about the birds and the bees, is it?"

"No," Bailey said, "it's not too late to talk about responsible sexual relationships. But you know, I think I'll do like you told me a few years ago and wait for that time when my husband and I discover each other on our marriage bed."

Early the next morning, Bertha woke her daughter. "Baby, you have a phone call. It's Xavier's mother."

Bailey got out of bed and went to the phone, concerned. "Hello? Mrs. Monroe, is everything alright?"

"Good morning, young lady. Just calm down, everything is fine. I just wanted to ask how did the move go?"

After a big exhale, Bailey told her future mother-in-law that everything went smoothly and that she'd planned to make the final move when she returned from the honeymoon.

"Why don't we get you moved into your new home today that will be one less thing to worry about?" Helen asked.

Bailey told Helen that she didn't have a key to the house, and Helen replied, "Well, I do. Victoria has talked to her husband, Caleb, and Olivia has convinced her husband, Trevor, to give us a helping hand. So they will be bringing the truck to your mother's house in an hour. Then we can get your things from there and from the storage unit and take them to your new home. See you soon."

As the wonderful lady disconnected the call, Bailey thought, *Okay, so that's who he gets his take-charge attitude from. She didn't even give me a chance to comment before she ended the call. Oh well, like mother like son.*

When the moving party arrived at Xavier's house and his mother was unlocking the doors, she looked at Bailey and bemoaned, "Young lady, I certainly hope that you give this place some personality. It's so cold and impersonal in here."

Helen was frowning as she stepped from the mud room into the kitchen. "Look at this place. He has nothing on the counters. A real kitchen has canisters and small appliances…and where are the curtains? How practical is it to have white shutter blinds in a kitchen?" She shook her head. "You know he never uses this place."

She clicked her tongue and walked through the butler's pantry into the dining room. "Look at this place. Not one doily, no tablecloth, no house plants anywhere. Oh, I can't stand it."

During the entire discourse, Bailey followed behind her future mother-in-law. "Mrs. Monroe, he's a man, and men don't think about the amenities that go into turning a house into a home."

Helen looked at her soon-to-be daughter-in-law. "I hope you continue to stay in his corner after you two have been married for a while." Hugging Bailey, she added, "You are just who he needs in his life, someone with unconditional love. Don't ever stop."

As the truck was unloaded, the ladies began to unpack Bailey's clothes and put them into the room-sized walk-in closet in the master bedroom. It didn't take more than an hour for the team of women to empty the boxes. Meanwhile, the men unloaded the few pieces of furniture that Bailey refused to sell when she moved and they placed them in the entry hall. Then they stacked the remaining pieces and boxes in the garage and left to return the truck.

As they took a final walk through the house, the ladies made suggestions to Bailey on how to make Xavier's house a more inviting place. For Bailey, it sounded like fun, but of course she wasn't going to make any changes without the approval of one Mr. Xavier Monroe.

It was early evening when Bailey was once again dropped off at her mother's house. Victoria reminded her that tomorrow was spa day, and Bailey smiled broadly. "Mother and I will be there. Have a good night, ladies." With that, she closed the car door and walked into her childhood home.

Chapter 21: Jumping Out of My Skin

Entering the reception lobby of Mr. Vinny's Spa, Bailey and Bertha were greeted by an extremely well-groomed man who stepped from behind the counter and said, "You must be members of the Anderson-Monroe party."

After they affirmed his assumption, he led mother and daughter into a dressing room.

Holding a clipboard, the man asked, "May I have your names, please?" Checking their names, he turned to Bailey. "So you're the miracle worker that's getting my friend back down that aisle. We're going to have to show you some extra attention as our way of saying thanks."

Surprised, Bailey smiled and nodded her head. "Okay, yes. That is me, I guess. Thank you."

He smiled and told the ladies that his name was Vincent but he was called Vinny by his friends, and that he had been one of Xavier's attendants at his first wedding. He then instructed them to go into the dressing rooms, take off their clothes, and get snapped into a bath sheet and a head wrap.

Bailey was warming to the idea of the spa treatment at Mr. Vinny's as soon as she was wrapped in the plush robe, fitted with a head wrap and a pair of very comfortable slippers, and shown to a room full of low-vibration recliners. The last amenity was lavender-infused moist heated towels on their faces.

After everyone had arrived, they were all led to the sauna for twenty minutes. After, they were escorted into a large room, also with vibrating reclining chairs, where their feet were wrapped in warm towels while their hands were soaked in warm, soapy water.

Each was given a chemical-free, lavender oil-scented mist steam facial treatment. After thirty minutes of pampering, they were taken to a room that had low lights, soft music, and five massage tables. Following a one-hour aromatherapy massage, they returned to the room with the vibrating recliners and finished their manicures and pedicures.

As the ladies left the spa feeling relaxed, they talked and laughed like lifelong friends. "That was a very interesting experience. Do you do this often?" Bertha asked Helen.

"Only when we can justify it to our husbands, girl," Helen said laughingly.

* * *

Early Friday morning, after tossing and turning all night, Bailey finally threw the covers back, climbed out of her bed, stumbled down the hall into her mother's room, and crawled into bed beside her.

Laying her Bible down, Bertha looked at Bailey and smiled. "Hello, little girl. Are you getting a little nervous?"

"Mom, it's Friday and I haven't heard anything about Xavier's interviews," Bailey said. "As a matter of fact, I haven't heard from him at all. I think I'm going to jump out of my skin if I don't hear something soon."

"Baby, its six o'clock in the morning. Give people a chance to wake up and get started for the day. Go back to sleep. Wait—I'll bet you haven't slept all night, have you?" Bailey shook her head. "Well, now, just go to sleep, young one. You don't want to get married tomorrow with puffy, sad-looking eyes." She reached over and rubbed Bailey's shoulders until she felt her daughter's body relax and heard her breathing softly.

By 11:30 in the morning, Bailey was on her way to the beauty salon and had still not heard from her fiancé. She was on pins and needles.

"If you don't stop squirmin' 'round like a three-year-old, you gonna get touched with this here hot comb!" Miss Aileen, the hairdresser, said to Bailey. "I know you don't wanna walk down that aisle with a big ol' burn mark on your neck."

"I'm sorry," Bailey said apologetically, "I'm a little anxious. It's just that I haven't seen Xavier in over a week, and I miss him."

Wow, she thought to herself, *did I just say that out loud?*

It was 1:15 when Bailey left the beauty salon. Her hair had been washed, hard pressed, curled tight, and tied in a silk scarf. Aileen reminded Bailey that she would be at her house at ten o'clock the next day to comb out her hair "so's you'll look fresh for the weddin'."

When Bailey walked through her mother's front door, Bertha asked her, "Are you feeling any better?"

Bailey shook her head. "Mom, I'm a bundle of nerves. I feel like I'm going to throw up."

"Well, don't do that," Bertha said. "You have company waiting for you in the living room."

Turning the corner from the foyer into the living room, Bailey prayed it wouldn't be Zane. "I'm so on the edge," she said to herself, "I don't think I can take any more surprises."

"I hope you can take just one more." It was Xavier.

Bailey wanted to run to him but her feet wouldn't move. She stood in the archway with her hands over her mouth and tears sliding down her cheeks.

He walked over to her, gently drew her into his chest, and held her until her silent sobs faded away. Cupping her face in his hands and wiping tears from her cheeks with the pad of his thumbs, he asked, "What is this all about?"

Looking up at him, Bailey realized the magnitude with which she had missed him. She realized that she was seeing him in another light because of the time they had spent apart. And the more she examined him, the more concerning the thoughts were that ran through her mind.

Why does his chest feel so good?
Has he always been such a hardbody?
Will his arms always feel this strong and comforting?
When did his eyes get so captivating?
Has he always smelled this good?

Biting her lip, she lowered her eyes to avoid the fact that she was staring at his full lips or into his sparkling brown eyes with the long, thick lashes. "I…uh…I'm glad to see you made it back safely," she said. "It has been a stressful week. How did things go for you?" Her throat was so dry that she was sure her voice sounded like a frog's croak.

For a moment, Xavier made no comment, looking down at this armful of woman with unconquered tight curves and eyes that looked at him like a deer caught in headlights. She looked so inviting with tears pooling in her eyes, making him want to be her champion and protector. He wanted to hold onto her, to continue to feel her full breasts rising and falling against the base of his chest, to keep his arms around her waist and let his hands rest in the arch at the base of her back, which blossomed into a full, firm, well-rounded mound.

Using almost all his self-control with a lot of regrettable effort, he dropped his arms and stepped back. "It's…um…" He cleared his throat. "It's good to be back. Things went well, I guess, because I made it to the finals. The announcements are going to be made on Tuesday night at a reception at the Hyatt Place. Would you mind if we pushed the honeymoon back a few days?"

Bailey shook her head. "I wouldn't mind at all. I really didn't even think we were going to have a honeymoon."

With that, Xavier nodded his head. "Okay, then. Thanks, Miss An— Uh…Bailey. I'll see you at church tomorrow, I hope."

To his own surprise, Xavier stepped forward and gave Bailey a quick hug, a kiss on the forehead, and a peck on each cheek. He held her hand as she walked him to the door. Just before he pulled the front door open, Xavier turned to look at Bailey.

"I missed you too," he said and pulled her close, kissing her until they both needed to take a breath. Then he determinedly pulled the door open and left.

Chapter 22: I Now Pronounce You…Married

Xavier stood beside his car outside the house where his wife-to-be was, looking at the horizon. His mind was in turmoil.

What just happened in there? he asked himself.

He could still feel Bailey's heat on his body, and it felt good. He could even still smell her hauntingly pleasant lavender scent. Most of all, he could still feel the tingle on his lips from that kiss.

He shook his head. "Snap out of it, man. Getting emotionally involved is not in the plans for now," he mumbled under his breath before he climbed into his car and drove home.

Bailey stood behind the door, looking through the window at her soon-to-be husband. She could still smell his woodsy-scented cologne and feel the rumble of his voice against her body as he cradled her softly and gently against his chest. Most of all, she could still feel the tingle from that kiss, and she liked it.

Snap out of it, girl, this is not the real deal. It's just a short-term arrangement! she mentally reprimanded herself.

Behind her, Bailey heard her mother chuckle. "I don't blame

you one bit for looking, baby. That truly is a *fine* young man. I like looking at him myself." She walked to her daughter's side and asked, "Now that you've seen him, do you feel better?"

Bailey took a deep breath and nodded her head. "Yes, now I feel better."

Bertha laughed again. "I know you do. I was watching the two of you, and I thought I was going to have to call the fire department to hose you both down."

"Mom," Bailey said, "I'm a little tired. I'm going to take a nap." She turned and ran up the steps to her bedroom, trying hard to ignore her mother's quiet laughter.

Later, that evening at around six o'clock, Bertha opened her front door to six women: Helen Monroe, Victoria Grayson, Olivia-Marie Williams, and Ja'Nell Bellison, as well as two other women who looked familiar although she couldn't remember their names. One lady was Delores, Victor's wife. The other was Kendra, Clayton's wife.

Bertha went upstairs and woke Bailey. Gently tapping her shoulder, she said, "Wake up, baby, you have company."

Bailey sat up slowly. "Who is it, Mom?"

"Just wash your face," Bertha said, "put on something casual and cute, and come on down."

As soon as Bailey walked into the room full of joyful women, she was fitted with a small veil and handed a glass of cranberry ginger ale.

"Now that the bride is here," Kendra said, "let the party begin."

The women were determined to have a good time at the small bachelorette party. "You can't have any alcohol," Olivia told Bailey. "You're getting married tomorrow. So we'll have a drink for you."

For the next few hours, the ladies laughed, talked, and shared relationship stories. Each told how it felt to them when they shared a *special time* with their husbands.

"Okay, Bailey," Victoria said with a wink, "you need to tell us if you and your future husband are compatible. How do you feel when you guys get close?"

Looking at each of the women, Bailey said, "I'm not telling you hens anything. You need to mind your own business."

"Look at that face!" Olivia said. "You can't fool us, girl. It must be good."

Everyone laughed, but Bailey still said nothing.

"Well, if you won't say anything, then I surely will," Bertha injected. "Xavier was here this afternoon. I think he had just gotten back into town, and judging from the smoldering embers that were being fanned in this room earlier today, well. Let me just say that I almost had to call the people who drive those big red fire engines, 'cause between the kissin' and hugging, it was gettin' hot all up in here!"

All eyes fell on Bailey, whose eyes flew open in surprised embarrassment. Her hands covered her mouth, and there was more than a hint of color in her cheeks.

It didn't help the situation very much for Bailey when Victoria pointed at the bride-to-be and said, "Look at you, acting just like a blushing bride."

Taking in their guest of honor, the women all laughed at her dismayed uneasiness.

*   *   *

On the morning of her wedding, Bailey got up extra early, got in the bath, moisturized and scented her body, and finally dressed in her bridal lingerie. Mary from Madam Ella's Bridal Shop, Miss

Aileen from the beauty salon, and Patricia, the first of three photographers, showed up right on time. Finally, the bridal party arrived and the pre-wedding preparations began.

Clayton Monroe, the best man, walked down the steps of the church and put his arm around Xavier's shoulder. "X? Brother, what are you doing out here?"

Xavier looked at his older brother. "The wedding is scheduled to begin at one o'clock and it's almost noon. Why aren't they here yet?" he asked slowly.

"Bailey does not strike me as the type of woman to stand a man up at the altar," Clayton said. "Besides, you know that women are always running a few minutes behind. Come on inside and let's take a breather before you have to get down that aisle."

The brothers walked back inside the Greater Metropolitan Community Church. The moment they disappeared into the building, a limousine pulled up to the curb and the bride and her party exited the vehicles, quickly entering the church through the side door.

The final minutes of bridal preparation were spent in the church's choir room. Final checks on makeup and hair were made before the veil was placed on Bailey's head and arranged over her face. Everyone hugged and kissed her.

Then, as the bride sat looking into the mirror and the photographer was taking her picture, Bertha said, "Goodbye, my precious little girl. When the veil is removed and I see your face again, you will be a married woman. May God bless you and the union richly."

Bailey kept her eyes on her mother's mirrored image as Bertha positioned the veil over her face. "Goodbye, Mommy, I love you."

At exactly one o'clock, "Always and Forever" by Luther Vandross began playing through the PA system. On cue, Pastor Jones, the groom, and his best man walked down the side aisles to the front of the church and stepped into place. Then, down the center aisle, the groom's parents were escorted in. Next, the bridesmaids in their lavender dresses with purple accents entered with the groomsmen in their black tuxedos with purple accents, followed by the ring bearer.

Ten minutes later, with everyone in place, the organist began playing the prelude to the wedding march. The white runner was rolled down the aisle, followed by the flower girl, who dropped purple, white, and lavender flower petals.

All of the wedding attendees stood and turned to see the bride step to the doorway and watched in awe as she was escorted down the aisle by her mother. Everyone marveled at how beautiful the bride looked, but no one was more surprised than the groom.

Bertha wore a lavender mother-of-the-bride dress with purple accents, while the bride wore a stark white strapless gown with a square cut form-fitting bodice that accented her full firm breasts, her small waist, and her well-rounded hips. The skirt of the dress was fitted to just below her hips, where it flared and flowed into a short train. The dress was accented with a full lace overdress with long sleeves that came to a point over her hands. Her short veil fell to her shoulders in the back and just under her chin in the front.

Pastor Jones announced, "We are all gathered to witness the union of Xavier Monroe and Bailey Marie Anderson."

When he asked who freely gave the bride to be married, Bertha announced, "Pastor Jones and witnesses: I, Bertha Anderson, freely and happily give my daughter to be married."

With that said, Xavier kissed Bertha on the cheek. An usher escorted Bertha to her seat, and the nuptials began.

The ceremony was not lengthy, but it was poignant and touching. The bride was nervous, and the groom held her hand gently but firmly, reassuring her there was no need to be apprehensive.

Bailey's wedding band was intricately complex. Xavier had to remove her engagement ring and slide it between the two connected diamond bands that completed the bridal set. This was when he realized he was a little nervous himself. It took him at least two minutes to link the rings and slide them on her finger with his trembling hands.

He knew it was going to be a double-ring ceremony, but he didn't know that his single-band four-diamond ring would be an exact masculine match to Bailey's rings. When the maid of honor handed his ring to the pastor, Pastor Jones blessed it and handed it to Bailey.

Xavier looked at his bride, smiled, and whispered, "Well, what is this?"

Offering a shy smile, Bailey didn't answer him but instead guided the ring onto his finger. Happily, his slipped on easily.

After affirming the importance of the rings and what wearing them symbolized, Pastor Jones concluded the ceremony with the instructions that everyone was anxiously awaiting: "Xavier, Bailey: I now pronounce you husband and wife. Mr. Monroe, you may salute your bride."

Xavier turned to Bailey and slowly lifted the veil. He smiled at her and quietly said, "Hello, Mrs. Monroe." Then he slid his arm around her waist, and with his other hand, he lifted her chin and kissed her lightly. As he pulled away, he whispered, "Thank you."

A chorus of oohs and ahhs floated throughout the church from the women who expressed their joy and happiness for the couple. Yet one woman did not. She stood unseen in the farthest recesses of the church. As she wiped a tear from her cheek she whispered, "This is not fair, Xavier. You didn't give me a second chance." Then she turned and quickly exited the building.

Looking pleased, Pastor Jones announced, "Ladies and

gentlemen, I present to you Mr. and Mrs. Xavier Monroe."

The couple turned to face their guests. They linked arms, walked down the three steps from the platform, jumped over the ornate broom, then strolled down the aisle through a bombardment of bubbles, out to their awaiting limousine. Standing at the doors of the sanctuary and snapping one picture after another was the second photographer, who had been taking still shots and also made a video of the entire service.

The reception was something else that Xavier was surprised about. "I thought we were going to wait to have a reception?" he spoke inquiringly.

"That's something you have to take up with the parents," Bailey told him. "The three of them got together, and they're giving this reception as one of their gifts to us. There was nothing I could do. You weren't here, and I couldn't fight that battle alone."

Xavier looked at his new bride, raised his hand, and gently smoothed the furrows between her eyebrows. "Well, in that case, let's enjoy the festivities."

A photographer was waiting for them at the Buxton Hotel, and he began taking pictures as the couple stepped from the limousine and continued throughout the afternoon and evening. He took pictures of the bride and groom in the receiving line; he took pictures of the couple leading the first dance, cutting the cake, and every other traditional shot he could get.

After all the guests had been served, the bride and groom were escorted to an overstuffed loveseat on a platform facing the reception area, where guests and family members toasted them, told stories about them, and presented them with gifts.

Then it was time for the first dance of the reception, to be led by the newlyweds. When they walked to the middle of the dance floor, "At Last" by Etta James began to play. The moment was electrifying for Bailey. Xavier himself didn't forget that this was just an act, but Bailey was so mesmerized by the intimacy of the moment that she forgot they were the center of attention. Her new husband pulled her close and looked deep into her eyes; her body trembled as she returned his gaze.

The women in the room all gasped as the groom gently guided Bailey's arms around his waist, cupped his bride's face in his hands, slowly raised her head, and intimately kissed her eyes, her cheeks, and finally her lips. With all of the sounds of approval from the guests, the couple at the moment didn't acknowledge anyone else's presence.

He smiled at her and whispered, "Don't look so frightened, Mrs. Monroe, it's going to be alright." Then he gave her a dazzling smile that was so infectious she couldn't help herself. She smiled back radiantly. Half the song had played before the other couples joined the swaying newlyweds on the dance floor.

After the dance, the couple posed by the cake and cut several slices that were served first to their parents and the bridal party members. The photographer's next-to-last picture was of the couple getting back into the limousine while guests cascaded them again with bubbles.

They were delivered by the limousine to 1964 Bluford Drive, their home together for the next two years. When the driver opened the car door, the photographer appeared and began snapping pictures of them up to the front door of the house. When Xavier opened the door, the photographer quickly stepped inside and said, "Let's do this the traditional way."

Xavier scooped Bailey up in his arms and carried her over the threshold. Surprised, he looked at the furniture that had been arranged in the entry hall. "Well, now, that's new," he said.

Bailey lifted her head and looked at him. "Is that a problem?"

He tightened his hold on her. "No. It looks nice."

"You were here yesterday. Is it the first time you've seen this?"

"Yes. I mostly use the back staircase coming into and going out of the house. I'm rarely in the front of the house unless I'm entertaining."

The photographer, recognizing the look of impatience from Xavier, quickly took the remaining shots and with a wide smile exited the newly coupled Monroe home.

Even though they were finally alone as he kicked the door closed, Xavier didn't set her down right away. The newlyweds stared at each other for a long moment before Xavier finally broke the silence. "I'm trying to decide. Do I carry you up the stairs, or do I let you walk?"

"I believe that I can make it up under my own power," Bailey said.

Putting her down, they walked side by side up the wide staircase. At the top, they stood gazing at each other. "We didn't talk about what would happen after the wedding, did we?" she asked.

"Well, we did once when we signed the contract," he offered, "but I'm not going to force anything. Let's just see how things develop."

Bailey readily agreed, and it seemed to release some of the tension that they each were feeling.

"Do you want to share a bedroom, or should we have separate rooms?" Xavier asked.

"That decision's up to you," Bailey replied, "it's your house. But as you can tell, we've been at your house recently. On Wednesday, your mother, your sisters, and I were here, along with your brothers-in-law Caleb and Trevor. Your mother and sisters put my clothes in the closet in the master bedroom. I didn't say anything because I didn't want to explain our arrangement to them."

When Xavier made no comment, Bailey studied her husband and thought she could see the strain on his face. "You know, Mr. Monroe, I think we should stay in separate rooms. You're a busy man and you need your privacy. I'll just go in and get something to sleep in tonight, and tomorrow I'll switch closets."

Looking somewhat surprised, Xavier made the final decision. "Well, this is your home too, at least for the next two years. So I say we share a bedroom, especially since your clothes are already there." Then, with a look of determination, he added, "The contract says that our arrangement will be a marriage in every sense of the word. Besides, the master suite has a king-sized bed. It's big enough for the two of us to stay away from each other if we want to."

After showering and getting into comfortable clothes, Xavier and Bailey met in the kitchen. She was pouring a glass of juice and making some toast when he came in. "I'm having a little bite," she said. "I was too nervous to eat during the reception. Would you like something, too?"

"Oh, so you *do* cook. I wasn't sure if you knew anything about the kitchen." When she gave him a hard look, he smiled and raised his hands in a surrender gesture. "I'll just have some juice."

They spent the rest of the evening sitting at the table making small talk, discussing things like their childhood, high school, and college experiences.

"I have to admit, you've had an exciting life compared to the experiences I've had," Bailey offered and then explained that after her father passed away, her mother was not eager to let her have a lot of freedom. She told him that her mother actually chose her prom dates for her.

When he heard that, Xavier laughed so hard that he had to stop and catch his breath. "I can't believe that I married a sheltered little mommy's girl. You have a lot of living to do in these next two years, young lady."

"Well, it's going to have to start tomorrow because I'm tired, and I'm sure you must be, too. This past week has been hectic for both of us."

Bailey pushed her chair away from the table, stood, put one hand on her hip, smiled provocatively, pointed at him with her other hand, and pronounced, "Just so you know, Mr. Monroe, I happen to be a *sassy* sheltered little mommy's girl. So watch what you say to me."

Xavier laughed and stood, but before he could comment, the doorbell rang. "You go on up, I'll get the door," Xavier instructed, and Bailey took the back staircase to the second floor. Just as she got to the door of the master bedroom, she heard loud arguing downstairs. She quickly walked to the main staircase and looked over the railing.

"Zane, she's my wife and I'm not going to argue with you about her intentions!" Xavier was saying. "She didn't trick me into anything. I *asked* her to marry me. And no, there is absolutely no way she could be pregnant. We got married because we wanted to, not because we had to. Now, big brother, I want you out of my house, and if you can't be civil to Bailey, then you are not welcome here!"

"See, she's already splitting us up and pushing us apart," Zane said as he raised his finger to point at Bailey. He swayed a little and continued with his allegations. "That's okay, baby brother, you'll see I'm right. She's no good for you. She's just a skanky, gold-digging tr—"

Without warning, Xavier hit his brother and laid him out on the floor of the entryway. Bailey ran down the stairs and stood between her new husband and her brother-in-law. Zane struggled to get up but couldn't seem to do it.

HOW

Xavier was preparing to hit his brother again if he continued maligning Bailey, his wife of only a few hours. Kneeling on the floor, Zane was holding his mouth, but he was still talking. "How can you do this to us? Why would you marry someone like her? What do you know about her, anyway? She's no good for you!"

Xavier raised his arm, but Bailey cried out, "No, stop! He's your brother!" She stepped closer to him and touched her hand to his chest. "Call your parents or your brothers and have someone come get him. I don't think he means any harm, he's probably just drunk."

Bailey's new husband looked at her intently, almost as if he was working at regaining a sense of balance and rationality. His arms were rigid, his hands were balled into tight fists, his eyes were glazed, and he was breathing heavily.

Without thinking, she stepped intimately close to Xavier and touched his cheek. "Xavier," she said in a near-whisper, "he's your brother."

Xavier blinked quickly and turned away from the sight of his brother cowering on the floor. He snatched up the telephone from its charger and dialed a number. "Clay, it's me. Can you come over? No, she's okay...it's not her. It's Zane. He came to my house all juiced up and talking crazy about my wife. I just punched him, and I just might do it again if somebody doesn't come and get him out of my house!"

Xavier's voice rose to a shout. When he spoke the last word, he didn't wait for an answer but simply ended the call and slammed the phone down. Bailey slid her arms around his waist and hugged him, partly to help calm him and partly to restrain him from going after his brother again, who by now was lying on his back on the floor.

Within twenty minutes, Clayton and Victor walked into the

kitchen from the garage while Bailey filled two insulated bags with ice cubes.

Clayton took one look at his new sister-in-law and asked two questions. "What happened? Are you alright?"

She nodded. "I'm fine, thank you." Her lower lip quivered when she said, "Xavier can tell you what happened. Zane is in the living room, and Xavier is pacing in the hall. He's so angry. I don't know what to do. I'm a little afraid. I've never seen Xavier act like that before." She looked at Clayton and Victor. "Can you take these in, please?" With trembling hands, she handed them the ice bags and ran up the back stairs.

Once inside the bedroom, Bailey pressed her back against the closed doors, trying to catch her breath and waiting for her heart rate to slow down. After about five minutes, she walked across the room, lay on the bed, and let the tears flow. She couldn't imagine why Zane had so much hatred for her.

Bailey heard the doorbell ring, but she didn't get off the bed. She thought it best if Xavier handled the situation. *This is my wedding night, and I'm crying. I should be happy. How did I get myself into this situation?* she thought.

Slowly, she turned to her side, pulled one of the bed pillows to her chest, and held onto it like it was her lifesaver. After dozing off and on for a while, she felt the bed sag behind her, and when she turned, she saw that it was her husband. Xavier could see by her red, puffy eyes that she was sad. He didn't say anything. He just folded her in his arms, cradled her to his chest, and they lay cuddled together in the middle of the bed for the rest of the night.

Chapter 23: Marriage is What You Make It

It was seven a.m. Sunday morning. Bailey woke to find herself in the arms of the man she had just married. And he was softly snoring. When she moved, he tightened his hold on her and opened his beautiful eyes. They looked so sexy up close like this.

"I...have to...get up," she said. He released his hold, turned over in the bed, and closed his eyes.

They had slept the entire night in each other's arms, in their clothes, on top of the bedcovers. She went to the bathroom and started the tub. Into the water, she measured out the bubbling bath oil, went into the closet, and took out a pair of lounging pajamas and matching slippers.

An hour later, after she had finished her bath, and with her body moisturized, she headed down to the kitchen to survey its layout. Once there, she found all the fixings for a light breakfast. Most importantly, she found a tea kettle, some tea bags, and two matching mugs.

When he felt something move beside him, Xavier had a moment of confusion. Then he remembered the wedding and the events that had occurred after the wedding ceremony. He quietly reflected on the sad scene that had faced him when he finally walked into the master bedroom on his wedding night. *Damn that Zane*, he thought.

He looked at the warm, soft, alluring creature lying against his chest and gazed into her mesmerizing eyes. They were big, sadly tender, and vulnerable, just like a newborn baby. He quickly released his hold on her and turned away. If he hadn't, their marriage would have quickly been consummated, and in a very unceremonious manner.

Later, standing at the kitchen door watching Bailey move around the room in those pink silky things she had on, he was amused. He had the urge to walk up behind her, turn her around, and kiss her until they were both senseless. Instead, Xavier cleared his throat and said, "Good morning. How long have you been up, and what are you doing?"

"Good morning yourself," Bailey said, beaming. "I've been up since seven o'clock, and it's called breakfast. I know a confirmed bachelor like you probably doesn't do breakfast, but I thought it would be a good icebreaker for the day after the wedding." Just then, the kettle whistled, and she reached over and poured hot water into two mugs.

The scent of brewing tea was interesting to Xavier. He pushed himself away from the door jamb, picked up a mug, and took Bailey's hand.

"I know what breakfast is, and even though I'm not a bachelor anymore, Mrs. Monroe, I believe I can still fix some breakfast for myself. Pick up your mug and let's get to the table. We have something to discuss."

He set his mug down, pulled out her chair, took her mug from her hand, set it on the table, and guided her into the seat. Without releasing her hand, he reached for her other one and sat in a chair in front of her.

"I want to apologize for what happened last evening. My brother is a drunken jerk. The family is meeting here today to talk about some options for getting him some help. But that plan is only going to move forward if you are okay with it."

Bailey kept her eyes down; if she looked at him, she knew she would surely lose her composure. "I don't have a problem with that. I can go to my mother's house until the meeting is over. I can only imagine the terrible emotional upset you all are feeling. I hope that no one is too upset with me. This is such a delicate situation. Some of your family members may be uncomfortable with me being here. I don't ever want to be a wedge between you and your family."

"You are not going anywhere, Bailey. You are family now, so this is your business too." Xavier gave her a tender half-smile. "Olivia and Victoria told me something happened at your apartment on Monday night, but they wouldn't tell me what. So I want to ask you what happened."

Reluctantly, Bailey told Xavier about the incident with Zane at her apartment. She felt his grip on her hands tighten slightly. His eyes darkened, his jaw clenched, and his nostrils flared—signs of anger and extremely good self-control. She concluded her recounting of the unpleasant occurrence by telling him that she'd used her stun gun on Zane. That made Xavier chuckle.

He leaned in and kissed Bailey softly on her cheek, trying to comfort her, then sighed despondently. "I'm sorry I wasn't there for you, but I promise you that as long as we are married, I have no intention of letting anyone or anything cause you to be unhappy. It's my intention that after today if my big brother doesn't get help, we don't ever have to associate with each other again."

At least for the next two years, he thought.

The newlyweds looked at each other pensively and slowly picked up their mugs.

Chapter 24: The House Becomes a Home

"You make a good cup of tea, Mrs. Monroe. I'm already ahead of the game. My bride can boil water for tea *and* make toast. What else can you cook? Or is this all there is in your recipe box?" Xavier asked lightheartedly.

"Oh, my goodness," Bailey said laughingly, "are you making a joke? I'll have you know that I'm a good cook! Just you wait. I'm going to make you a meal today that will amaze you. We can start with the breakfast casserole that's in the oven."

Thirty minutes later, breakfast was over and Bailey was washing the dishes. "There's a dishwasher, you know," Xavier said. "And yeah, the breakfast was good. But even I can make something that resembles breakfast in a pinch." He started drying the dishes and putting them away.

"I can't believe you're trying to tell jokes. I've never seen you smile so much."

"What do you mean you've never seen me smile? I'm a fun-loving guy. I smile all the time. Just you wait, you'll see."

Bailey loved the way his face lit up when he smiled. She thought he was even more handsome when he was relaxed and enjoying himself. Watching him and enjoying the lighthearted, almost joyful time they were spending together, Bailey mused to herself, *I could fall deeply in love with this man.*

Knowing that her train of thought was nothing more than wishful thinking, she asked, "What time is everyone coming?" She did it to take her mind off the fact that this handsome man was her husband, and he was standing way too close.

"About 2:30, after church," he told her.

"Well, what are you going to do until then?"

"I don't know. What do you have in mind?"

She asked him to help get some of the boxes out of the smaller garage that she had stored there on Wednesday afternoon. Then she offered, "You look a little tired. After you finish getting those boxes for me, why don't you go up and take a nap?" And that was just what he did.

During the next few hours, Bailey unpacked her knickknacks and set about making her new husband's house look like a home. In the dining room, she covered the table with a burgundy tablecloth. Over that, she placed an off-white, heavy French lace tablecloth. In the middle of the table, she set a thirty-inch round wooden candleholder base plate that was topped with an etched crystal globe. On the plate, inside the globe, she put a large four-wick, white lavender scented candle.

The living room was an expansive space well-lit by a wall of windows that were covered with expensive, pinch-pleated drapes over several pairs of beige sheers topped with waterfall valances. The adjoining wall was covered with stained rock and housed an oversized fireplace with an extra-long, heavy oak mantel stretching across the top of the entire open space.

The room's last two walls were painted medium tan; one was

interrupted by the archway, and the other became the resting place for her large, framed mirror with a matching dark cherry wood double-door half-moon table. She liked the way everything looked in that space, so right away she placed a round Nottingham lace scarf on the table and topped it with a three-piece set of crystal candle holders.

Just to add a little more of her feminine touches, Bailey covered the middle of the coffee table with a Nottingham lace runner. On it, she placed a fluted leaf-etched crystal bowl that she filled with heavily scented lavender potpourri. On each side of the bowl, she placed the matching fluted candle holders that contained lavender and chamomile-scented candles. On the mantel, she arranged a dozen multicolored, multi-scented votive candles in fluted votive candle cups.

The entry hall was divided by the staircase; the right side was the narrow side and led to the guest coat closet. Bailey thought this would be a good place for her iris-dome floor lamp. She ran to the garage to get the lamp and decided to take the frameless wall mirror with matching etchings to hang next to the lamp in that alcove. After hanging the mirror and positioning the lamp, she was pleased with the light that made the space look cozy. She hoped Xavier would like it also.

The left side of the entry hall was wide enough to serve as a small sitting room. This side was furnished with her two Queen Anne chairs on the long wall separated by a low table with a land-line telephone on it, and on the opposite wall was the matching loveseat. She liked the way it looked, so she let them stay there exactly where her brothers-in-law had placed them.

Bailey centered a short Battenberg lace runner on this table and placed a crystal pencil/pen holder on the runner along with one of their wedding gifts, a crystal picture frame that had a very small X

Monroe engraved in each corner.

At the end of this side of the entryway was a swinging door that led to the kitchen. She stepped through the doorway and stood there for a few minutes. Then she walked into the pantry to see what there was for her to cook. She wanted to prepare a meal that would dazzle Xavier for doubting her culinary skills.

In the pantry, she found several golden-skinned potatoes, onions, and the seasonings she needed. In the freezer, she found a nice boneless prime rib roast. When everything had been assembled, she began the preparation for an amazing dinner. She flash-thawed the roast, dressed it, and put it into the oven at 350 degrees. In the refrigerator, she found some fresh broccoli, a small head of cauliflower, and a variety of cheeses. This dinner was really going to be good.

While she was waiting for the roast to start cooking, she placed the last of her knickknacks around the kitchen. She had a dozen angels, so she put the heavenly choir on top of the refrigerator, the angel family in the middle of the kitchen table, and the sandbox angels on the windowsill. When that was done, she started on the side dishes that would accompany the prime rib roast.

Finishing the preparation for dinner, Bailey couldn't believe that it was almost 1:30, but she had spent her time productively, had added a few feminine touches to a couple of rooms, and had prepared a medium well-done, horseradish-crusted prime rib roast, a pot of creamy garlic ranch potatoes, and a cheesy broccoli, carrot, and cauliflower casserole.

"Let's see him joke about my cooking skills now," she said as she walked up the back staircase and quietly eased her way into the bedroom, intending to take a quick shower to freshen up and dress before members of the Monroe family arrived.

"Just what were you doing down there all this time?" Xavier

asked. He was sitting in an overstuffed leather reclining chair watching a football game.

"I thought you were asleep. Is this a good game?" she replied without answering his question.

He returned the recliner to its upright position and stood. "I dozed off and on, but I couldn't sleep, and this is what I do to relax. What were you doing down there for five hours?"

"Are you nervous about the announcement for the district attorney position? Is that why you can't sleep?" Bailey asked.

He walked over and stood directly in front of her. "That's the second time you have not answered my question. Are you trying to hide something?"

Stepping back, she said, "No, I have nothing to hide. But if you want to see what I've been doing, you should go down and see for yourself." She had a faint smile on her face, and that made him more curious.

"Okay," Xavier said, taking her hand, "but you're coming with me. You didn't tear down any walls, did you?"

They descended the main staircase, and once they were at the bottom, he turned to her and asked, "Okay, now what?"

Bailey led him across the entry hall into the dining room, where they stood in the arched doorway and looked at the room. Surprised, he commented, "It looks nice, and I like that scent."

She smiled, turned, and walked across the entryway, leading him into the living room. She stood beside him and looked around the room again. When she looked up at him, he was smiling.

"That's the same scent, just a little more intense," he said. "And it looks nice in here, too. Wow, it looks like a woman lives here, and I didn't have to take out any walls."

Bailey led him back out into the entryway.

"This looks nice too, and I see that you've incorporated some other little accents along with your furniture in the decorating." He sniffed the air. "But the air smells differently. That's not a scent, it's an aroma. Did you cook something?"

She led him into the kitchen and walked around the island to the stove. She opened the oven door and lifted back the covering on the roast. Xavier looked at her and smiled. After basting the meat, she closed the oven door and raised the tops from the pot of potatoes and the casserole dish.

"Okay," Xavier said, "I guess I owe you an apology. You can cook much more efficiently than I thought earlier." He stepped close to her and pulled her into his arms, but before he could reward her with a kiss that would have rendered them both senseless, the front doorbell chimed and they jumped away from each other like two teenagers caught kissing.

"I'll get it," she said, but he touched her arm.

"No, you should go get out of those little silky things, and I'll answer the door." As Bailey turned to walk away, he gave her a light swat on her rear end. "We can pick up where we left off later." He laughed and walked into the entry hall while she bounced up the stairs.

"This better be somebody special," Xavier whispered to himself, shaking his head. "I was about to make my move on that woman."

Michael and Michele, Clayton and Kendra's three-year-old twins, ran to their uncle when he opened the front door. They each grabbed a leg and together begged, "Give us a ride, Uncle Xavier."

Clayton and Kendra were both carrying storage containers, and each had thermal bags swinging from their arms. "The caterer bagged this food up last night for you and Bailey, but we wanted to give you two some privacy, so here is everything now," Clayton explained.

When Xavier turned to walk into the living room with a child riding on each leg, Kendra said, "Wait a minute, what happened in here? This house looks different, and it has scents and aromas in it. What's going on? Where's my new sister-in-law? I can't wait to see what she looks like on the day after her wedding."

"Hello to you too, Kendra," Xavier said. "She'll be down in a little bit. Have a seat. I'll go get her. Let me have those bags. Make yourself comfortable."

While Kendra was peeling her twins from Xavier's legs, Clayton asked, "How is she doing today, X? Zane said some pretty harsh things about her last night. Is she alright?"

"Last night," Xavier said, "I felt that if Zane wasn't my brother, I would have killed him. Because of his crazy behavior and harsh words, Bailey cried herself to sleep. He not only hurt her but he hurt me. I don't know what his problem is, but right now I'm feeling like I don't want to see him again."

Kendra offered, "Wait. Please don't feel that way. He's still your brother."

"I know, Kendra, that's what Bailey kept telling me last night, even while he was saying those hateful things about her." He looked at his brother and sister-in-law and added, "I'll be right back. I'm going to go up and check on her."

By the time Xavier walked into the bedroom, Bailey was exiting the closet fresh from her shower and fully dressed, much to his chagrin.

"Who was at the door?" she asked.

"Clayton and his family. They came with the leftover food from our reception. His wife's name is Kendra, remember? And they have three-year-old twins, Michelle and Michael, and those two little ones have a lot of energy." Looking at her wistfully, he added, "That was a quick change. I was coming to give you some help."

"I don't need any help right now," she said, grinning, "but if you want to change your clothes, I'm here to help you."

"Well, now, I would love to take you up on that offer, but it will have to wait until later. For right now, I'll settle for this." He pulled her close enough for full-body contact, embraced her so tightly that nothing was left to the imagination, and kissed her until they were both in desperate need of air. Bailey closed her eyes and laid her head on his chest, enjoying the feel of his arms and the beat of his heart as she tried to regain her sense of balance.

Xavier wrapped his arms tightly around her, trying to regain control of his mind and his body. He whispered to himself, "Man!"

Bailey inhaled deeply, cleared her throat, and spoke softly, "Xavier, there's something that I need to tell you, but I don't quite know how."

He leaned back to look at her. He could feel that she was tense. "This must be serious. You'd better tell me."

She stepped away from him and looked down at the floor. "I...um...I know that you want to consummate this marriage, but... I've never had sex before."

She didn't look up until she heard him whisper, "You're a virgin?" Then he smiled.

"You're not upset?" she asked.

He shook his head. "No, not at all. I think it's quite refreshing. When everyone leaves tonight, you'll have to tell me how you managed to maintain that status for so long."

The doorbell chimed as Bailey and Xavier were walking down the steps. They answered it together. It was Victor, his wife, Delores, and their daughter, Monette. The next people to arrive were Trevor and Olivia and their four teenagers, Dalton, Peter, Vashti, and Garrett. They were followed by Judge and Helen Monroe, who were delivering the top layer of the wedding cake. The last of the

Monroe family members to arrive were Caleb and Victoria with their son, Timothy.

After receiving her welcoming kiss from Xavier, Helen looked around and immediately commented on the changes. "It looks, feels, and smells like a woman lives in this house." Then she turned to regard Bailey. "Daughter-in-love, show me what you've done."

Helen handed the cake to Xavier and gestured for the other women to follow her and Bailey as they surveyed the changes she had made to the house. All of the women had brought a dish or two of food with them, and even though Xavier and the other men had put everything in the kitchen, inevitably, the women's tour ended there.

"It smells divine in here, what did you cook?" Kendra asked.

Bailey uncovered everything and asked the ladies to help her prepare the tables. She asked her mother-in-law to slice the roast and prepare the au jus. Then she asked Olivia and Victoria to reheat the family contributions, the reception leftovers, and the rest of the dinner she had cooked, and place everything on the counters.

Kendra and Delores prepared coffee and lemonade, put the plates and utensils on the island, and within forty-five minutes, the Monroe family had eaten and enjoyed the first meal that the new Mrs. Monroe had prepared in her new home.

Chapter 25: Taming the Stallion

It was three hours after everyone's arrival when Xavier walked into the kitchen with the glasses and cups he had collected. The ladies stopped talking.

The family had completed their meeting and had come to a decision about dealing with Zane. It was decided that the brothers would meet with Zane and encourage him to check himself into a rehab facility for his alcohol addiction. They were determined to let him know that in his present condition, he was not only harming himself but causing his loved ones sadness and heartache. They would assure their oldest sibling that no matter how long it took him to recover, they would be part of his support team.

Xavier set everything on the newly cleaned island and stepped to Bailey. "Excuse us, ladies, I want to talk to my wife."

He touched Bailey in the arch of her back and they walked into the butler's pantry.

In a whispered voice, he said, "I don't know about you, but I'm ready to tell these people to get out of my house. We have some things we want to do." Then, smiling at his wife, he pulled her close and kissed her passionately.

When they came out of the pantry and Xavier walked out of the kitchen, Olivia turned to Bailey and asked, "What were you two doing in the pantry?"

She laughed. "Nothing. He had something to tell me, that's all."

Victoria chuckled. "Well, the next time you two *talk*, tell him not to be so enthusiastic, girl. Your lips are puffy, and those eyes of yours are sparkling."

Kendra smiled, twirled her hand in the air, and asked, "So how does it feel being the one who tamed the wild stallion? Ride 'em, cowgirl! Yeehaw!"

With that, the women broke into laughter and Bailey blushed, which made them laugh even harder.

Later, while her husband was securing the house, Bailey managed to get in and out of the shower. She combed her hair, put on her nightgown, and dabbed on a light fragrance just as he came into the bedroom.

After Xavier had taken a quick shower in the guest bathroom, he returned to the master suite and stood waiting for his wife to finish her shower. When Bailey slowly walked out of the bathroom, the lights had been turned off and a few of the votive candles from the living room mantel were lit and set around the bedroom. Soft music was playing.

Xavier stood before Bailey and looked down at her tenderly. In a slow, seductive motion, he lifted her off her feet and gently placed her on the bed. Lying on his side and looking at Bailey with his head propped on his elbow, Xavier said, "You are a very appealing woman. You are so attractive. It's easy to see that you take care of yourself, and you always smell so clean and fresh and sexy. You are independent, resourceful, and even a little feisty. There are so many things about you that I want to learn. Let's start with how you managed to keep your virginity—until now, that is."

"It's really very simple. My mother was very protective, and the boys at school and at church were afraid of her. Not many boys wanted to date the vice principal's daughter or the daughter of the Sunday school superintendent. So since no one ever asked me for a date, I was focused on school, and my entertainment was reading, studying, and watching movies with my mother. The two dates I've had in my life were with boys she selected and at dances she chaperoned."

Xavier sat up and looked at his new wife. He had a broad smile on his face and chuckled. "You are so amazing and full of surprises." He touched her shoulder lightly with his finger and felt her shudder. Immediately, he reached out with both hands and lifted her onto his lap. "Are you cold?"

She shook her head. "Just a little nervous. I've never been so close to a man before."

"Really?" Xavier asked.

"You know, I mean, like this. Intimately." She touched his cheek and looked into his eyes. "I'm at the point of no return, and I don't have any idea what to do."

Hugging her, Xavier said, "Well, just let me take the lead. You hold on, because we're about to get genuinely intimate. And I think we are both going to enjoy ourselves."

Xavier was true to his word, and for the next hour, he warmly cuddled, caressed, stroked, kissed, and embraced every part of his new wife's body.

"You're a real trooper, Mrs. Monroe," Xavier said to Bailey as they soaked in the tub. "It won't be so uncomfortable next time. I promise."

She gave him a weak smile. "If you say so, Mr. Monroe. I guess I have to believe it. But just so you know, it did eventually become more enjoyable than I expected."

He looked at her compassionately as he sponged warm, soapy

water over her shoulders and down her arms. He remembered the tears she'd tried to hide when their bodies joined together for the first time. "You know, it's your fault that I couldn't wait any longer to consummate our union."

"My fault? How are you blaming me for surrendering my virginity to you?" she asked with a frown.

"Yes, it's your fault. You are a beautiful, sexy woman, and in case you don't know it, girl, your body is incredibly inviting. It feels good…too good. It's soft. Smooth. It's full and curvy in just the right places. Even the way you move is captivating and appealing. Then on top of that, you walked around this house in those little pink silky things all morning, seductively begging me to snatch you and drag you to bed. So, yes, it's your fault."

There was nothing she could say except, "You really feel that way about me?"

"Yes, and stop giving me those wide-eyed innocent looks or we'll be making love again, only this time, I won't be so considerate!"

She looked at him and smiled. "Do it."

He stood up and pulled her with him. He snatched a towel from the warming rack and wrapped her in it. He grabbed another one and wrapped it around his waist. Helping her out of the tub, he threw her over his shoulder, slapped her on her rear end, and carried her to bed.

Waking up in a man's arms was strange for Bailey, and it was even more astonishing to awaken in the arms of the man she'd had romantic thoughts about for years. And for him to be her husband was almost unbelievable for one Bailey Anderson-Monroe.

She moved away from his chest, and his arms tightened. "Don't leave me," he whispered, "I like the way you feel."

The newlyweds made love twice more before they left the bed.

"I'm so sorry, I know that you are probably uncomfortable, but I can't get enough of you," the newly married lawyer said sensuously to his wife.

Chapter 26: The Appointment

Bailey got out of bed an hour after she woke.

"We should get changed and packed as soon as we can," Xavier said to her. "We have an eighty-five-mile drive to Des Moines. I want us to get there today and be settled before the banquet begins tomorrow."

"Xavier, do you think you are one of the appointees?" she asked him.

"I certainly hope so. There were three positions open: the state district attorney, and two assistant district attorneys. I'd be happy with either one of the assistant positions but even happier to get the DA's job."

The drive to Des Moines was interesting. The main topic of conversation was whether big brother Zane would voluntarily admit himself to the area rehabilitation hospital or if he would force the family to get a court order to commit him.

Xavier told Bailey what his parents and siblings had decided to do about Zane. "Our parents decided that Clayton and Victor would go to Zane and tell him about the family's decision, and that was a plan we all agreed with."

Continuing, Xavier explained that they would tell Zane the

family would give him a week to make his decision or they'd get a court order and assume responsibility for him and his wellbeing.

Bailey asked Xavier why his brother was convinced she was such a negative influence on him. Xavier told her he had no clue, but what he did know was that Zane had a problem with overconsumption of alcohol.

"And I intend to keep my promise to you," Xavier said. "If he says anything about you again or totally loses his mind and tries to confront you, or if he ever puts his hands on you again, I'm going to forget he's my big brother."

"Xavier, I really don't want to be a dividing factor in the family. I don't think anything or anyone should come between siblings."

Xavier patted her on the knee. "You are absolutely right. But neither anything nor anyone should come between a husband and his wife, either." He was surprised to hear those words come from his mouth. He pulled his hand away and focused his eyes on the road.

Bailey was also surprised, so much so that she had nothing to say. She looked at Xavier and smiled appreciatively at him. They drove the last twenty-five miles of the way in silence, letting the soft sound of music fill the car.

They checked into the Hyatt Place Hotel in downtown Des Moines. Bailey looked around the hotel atrium while Xavier completed the registration. She noticed a woman watching them intently from across the lobby. It was the same stunning woman from the reception at the Plaza. When she turned to ask Xavier if he knew the woman, the woman quickly exited through the main doors and rounded the corner before he could turn and look, ignoring the doorman's offer to flag her a taxi.

The couple spent the rest of the afternoon exploring the city. They toured the African American Historical Museum and the gardens at the Botanical Center.

"Let's go back to the hotel," Xavier whispered into his wife's ear, standing behind her with his arms around her waist. "I want to find out how that bed feels."

Bailey turned her head, looking pleasantly surprised. "I thought you would never ask. Let's go, big boy. After all, this is supposed to be our honeymoon."

"Well, now, Mrs. Monroe, how you do go on," Xavier whispered. They both laughed and walked out of the gardens holding hands.

They were so focused on each other that they were unaware of being watched. The lone figure stood in the shadow of a very large tropical plant. She watched the departing couple and smiled in a most sinister fashion. "Enjoy him now, Miss Bailey Anderson," she said under her breath, "because soon, he's going to be all mine again."

Xavier and Bailey made a handsome couple as they entered the Hyatt Place banquet hall. He wore a custom-made tuxedo; she wore a mauve, strapless cocktail dress with a full-flowing skirt accentuated with a black sequin bow belt. The dress was topped with a sheer black sequin-trimmed shrug jacket. Adding to Bailey's appearance was her hair. She once again had forgotten how she usually kept it in a single braid that she wound into a ball at the base of her head. For tonight, her husband had convinced her to wear her hair loose in a straw curl style. It was very attractive and gave her an enchanting allure. As they walked into the banquet room, many of the guests gave the couple more than a passing look.

When they checked in at the registration counter, Bailey and Xavier were escorted to their table, but rather than being seated, Xavier decided to walk around and get acquainted with some of the other guests. Bailey watched her husband circulate around the room, socializing, admiring not only his masculine appeal but his straightforward and effortless demeanor with the other guests.

After dinner, the lieutenant governor gave a short speech about the importance of the position of the state's district attorney and the assistant DAs. At the conclusion of his talk, Lieutenant Governor Aaronson announced that Amanda Clarks had been selected for the position of second assistant DA and that the position of first assistant DA had been awarded to Beryl Thomlin.

Bailey slid her hand from her lap to reach over and lightly squeeze Xavier's thigh as a gesture meant to comfort and fortify her husband. He covered her hand with his. When his name was announced as the new state district attorney, he squeezed back and kissed her cheek before walking to the platform to be formally introduced to the audience.

For the rest of the evening, Bailey stood back with a smile and watched her husband accepting his congratulatory acknowledgments. As she was having her wine glass refilled, someone effortlessly slid into the chair next to her. When she turned, she was looking directly at the woman from the reception at the Plaza—the one who had tried to cause her to fall during her morning jog; the stunning woman from the hotel lobby.

"Yes, can I help you?" Bailey offered with a subdued smile.

The woman had a smirk on her face. "Let's not play games. I'm sure you know who I am. My name is Priscilla Grayson. I'm Xavier's first and only true love. And so, Miss Anderson, I won't waste your time or my words. We both know that Xavier only married you because he thought he couldn't have me. You can't believe that he would actually choose someone like you over me. Let me assure you that if I had been here, he would never have given you as much as a second thought."

"Miss Grayson," Bailey replied, "you may call me Mrs. Monroe.

And this is what I want you to remember. *He* asked *me* to marry him ten years after you walked away. If you had not run away, this whole conversation would not be happening. So now, what can I do for you tonight?"

"That's all well and good, *Mrs. Monroe*, but you remember this. Getting him is easy. Keeping him is another set of circumstances altogether. And I'm making it my duty to let you know my intention is to be Mrs. Xavier Monroe if it's the last thing I do."

Bailey said, "Miss Grayson, I have no intention of fighting over any man, including the one I'm married to, so if you want to make a fool of yourself, then have at it. Just remember, whatever happens, I'll always be the first Mrs. Xavier Monroe simply because I *didn't* leave him standing at the altar."

Xavier looked across the room and couldn't believe what he was seeing. What was Priscilla doing here? He excused himself from the group and began to walk toward the table. Just as he reached his destination, Priscilla Grayson stood and turned to him.

He stepped back and greeted her. "Hello, Priscilla. It's been a while. How have you been? I see you've met my wife?"

"Hello, and congratulations on your appointment, Skippy. And yes, we've met." Priscilla scowled at Bailey and slid her hand down Xavier's' arm. "It's good to see *you* again, Skippy. Let's get together. Soon." Then she turned and sauntered away.

Chapter 27: Living Life as a Couple

For the rest of the week, Xavier was involved in meeting his staff and reviewing the active cases that were being left behind by his predecessor. This meant that for the major portion of every day, Bailey was on her own.

Not being one to sit idle, she left the hotel and explored the metropolitan community. She meandered her way through the city's downtown business and shopping districts; she ate a light lunch at a table by the city center fountain and watched the ebb and flow of the daytime downtown life of the city center in Des Moines.

On Friday evening during rush hour, the Monroes drove back home. "I wanted to see how it will be to make this commute every day," Xavier explained. "An almost two-hour daily commute is not something I would want to do by car."

"Well, are you interested in living in the city?" Bailey asked. "I wouldn't want you to be on the road for so long every day, either. Especially in the evenings after a long, hard day at work."

"If you're there waiting at the door for me, it'll make it all worthwhile," Xavier teased.

Bailey looked at him with a smile playing on her lips. "Of course if that's what you want, then that's what I'll try to give you. You just be careful."

"Don't worry," he said with a smile, "you know there's train service from Creston to Des Moines. I plan to take the commuter to the city and then ride the shuttle to the office. So, Mrs. Monroe, the problem is solved, and there's nothing about this that you should worry about."

* * *

Life for Xavier and Bailey settled into a workable routine. During the week, they awoke at 5:30 a.m. to get prepared for the day and have breakfast together. By 7:00 a.m., Xavier was on the commuter station platform waiting for the 7:15 to Des Moines. By 8:40, he was exiting the shuttle at the state justice building, walking into his office five minutes later.

In the meantime, after bidding her husband goodbye, Bailey would clean the kitchen, dust and vacuum one of the rooms, straighten the bedroom, and get dressed to go to the Jackson and Monroe offices.

There was a new associate at the office who had been hired just after Xavier's appointment as the district attorney. Marie Jackson was Alexander Jackson's sister, and she was just as efficient but definitely not as easygoing as her brother. She didn't seem to care for Bailey Anderson-Monroe, the office manager and lead office administrator, or Ja'Nell Bellison, the office receptionist and basic skills tech specialist.

Marie Jackson often looked for but seldom found mistakes that Bailey or Ja'Nell made. She frequently demanded they provide her with certain amenities, like a cup of coffee, a glass of juice, or a thermos of iced, bottled water prepared for her when she entered the office. She even asked them to go out and get her lunch, and even made attempts to have them do her personal shopping for her.

The third weekend in March was the newlywed's six-month anniversary, and Bailey informed the associates and Ja'Nell that she'd be leaving early that Thursday and would not be back in the office until the following Tuesday.

Marie Jackson felt that Bailey "had no right to shortchange them for her own personal reasons" and voiced her opinion at the Monday morning staff meeting. When no one agreed with her, she tried to make Bailey's day very unpleasant.

When Ja'Nell was at lunch, Marie summoned Bailey to her office over the interoffice messenger, writing *Bailey, get in here now!*

Bailey returned the message, writing *I'm sorry, Ms. Jackson. Ja'Nell is out of the office right now. I can't leave the reception area. What can I do to help you?*

Instead of answering the message, the attorney angrily stormed out of her office, down the hall, and into the administration center. "You no-good piece of trash," she snarled, "when I tell you to do something, you do it right away! You don't give me any excuses. Do you understand me?" With that, she threw several sheets of paper at Bailey and snapped, "Get this typed and back to me in an hour!"

Her voice was so loud that Alexander Jackson stepped out of his office to see his sister throw the papers at Bailey. Then he watched Bailey gather the papers and slowly stand.

"Hold it, ladies, what is the problem here?" Alexander asked.

"I want her fired!" Marie said. "She's incompetent and insolent."

"What are you talking about?" he said. "She has been our office manager for over eight years, and no one has ever had any complaints about her, so you will have to share your reasons for these outrageous charges."

"Over eight years, really? Perhaps she's gotten a little too comfortable and it's time she started looking for a new job. She's audacious and disrespectful. She doesn't follow instructions. She avoids working with the associates and shirks her duties onto others. She doesn't demand the proper respect from that gutter-snipe receptionist, and she doesn't give the proper respect to her superiors. Besides all of that, she must think that being married to one of the partners gives her special privileges."

Andrew looked at his sister angrily. "You know, Marie, I think the one who should be terminated is you. If you can't get along with these two women, then it's you who has the problem, not them. I won't allow you to disrespect Mrs. Monroe or anyone else in this office. Now I'm going to give you the rest of this week off to make up your mind. Don't forget that I'm the one who determines who does and does not work in these offices."

"Alex, are you firing me? Are you choosing her over me, your own sister?"

"Marie, this has nothing to do with family relationships. This is a business, and I can't afford to have dissension and strife in this workplace. No, I'm not firing you. I'm suspending you for improper conduct. I've heard how you've treated my staff and heard the ridiculous demands you've tried to put on them. I've also noticed how you try to undermine their performance. So be thankful that I'm only suspending you, because if I fired you, I'd have to give a reason, and that would hinder your ability to get hired by another firm."

Without another word, Marie turned and walked quickly to her office, her brother right behind her. "Marie," he said, "you have been a spoiled brat since we were children. Nobody here is going to pamper you, so when you return from your suspension, I certainly hope that you have adjusted your attitude, or my next step will definitely be to terminate you."

Alexander returned to the administration center after having escorted his sister out the back door. "My sister has been unpleasant since we were children, but I thought she had grown out of it. I'm sorry you had to experience that."

"Mr. Jackson," Bailey said, "please don't fire her. She's a good attorney, and I would hate for her to have a termination on her résumé. Let us sit down together when she returns, and maybe we can work something out between the two of us."

"It's a deal, young lady. Now what do you have planned for that six-month anniversary?"

"Not much. I just want to spend a day with my husband, family members, and some friends. We'll probably have a meal and some entertainment. Are you and Melody coming?"

Andrew nodded enthusiastically. "Yes, we are coming. We've waited for so long to see Xavier in the position of being a happily married man."

Chapter 28: Falling

Xavier enjoyed walking into his home every night and being greeted by a charming, attractive woman who had the house filled with the mouth-watering aromas of a home-cooked meal. He especially enjoyed the calm, quiet atmosphere. He appreciated the fact that his wife respected his space and didn't stress him with boring recounts of her day. He liked the way she listened to him and didn't try to take over the conversation when they talked.

It was evident that Bailey had worked hard to give his house some personality and make it look and feel comfortable, inviting, and warm. Even his mother approved of the changes, and she never failed to mention it when she was visiting.

On occasion, he had to remind himself this was not a permanent arrangement, and that this was also not a genuine marriage. It was a relationship that was more like "friends with benefits." He had to admit, however, that it was good to have that warm, supple, responsive body next to him in the middle of the night, in the morning, and even during the weekend afternoons.

That was why he had to occasionally withdraw from her presence and lock himself in the den, even when he really didn't have any work to do, otherwise, he'd spend all of his time with her, falling into something that he couldn't get out of.

Admittedly, it was going to be uncomfortable when it came time to dissolve the marriage, but he was sure he would get over it—in all actuality, he reasoned, this relationship was really nothing more than just a contractual agreement.

On Friday, Xavier called Bailey to let her know he was taking a later train and wouldn't get home until 7:45. She didn't seem to mind and told him she would see him when he got home. She even asked him if he had eaten and if there was anything special he wanted for dinner.

One day for real, she is going to make someone a truly good wife, Xavier thought to himself as he ended their conversation.

When he finally pulled into the driveway, Bailey was standing in the mud room, waiting for him to get out of the car. She had an expression on her face like she was glad to see him. She looked so inviting.

"Hello," she said, " welcome home. I'm glad you made it. Do you want a shower or a bath?"

"You, right now. I want you in the shower. How does that sound?"

"That sounds good to me, but we're having company tonight. And, by the way, happy six-month anniversary!" Bailey took him by the hand and led him into the kitchen where she had prepared the prime rib roast meal she'd cooked the day after their wedding. Xavier's mouth watered.

"Who's coming over?" he asked, slightly perturbed. "I thought we could have a quiet evening and a late morning."

"Xavier, I'm sorry. I wanted to have a little celebration tonight and have tomorrow all to ourselves. I wanted to surprise you. I didn't think that you would have an extended day. It's a little too late to try calling it off."

"Are you saying we can have a late morning? As in we stay in bed until noon?"

She laughed. "As in you stay in bed until noon and I'll make you breakfast. We can have breakfast and a movie in bed if you want."

He drew her into the circle of his embrace. She was full and curvy in the right places, she smelled so good, her mouth was warm and inviting, and she was quickly receptive to his kiss and responsive to his touch.

"Knock, knock," someone said. "Excuse us, we were invited, but we can turn around and come back later." Clayton and Kendra were standing in the mud room holding a cake, and behind them were the rest of the guests.

"Well, since you're already here, you may as well come in," Xavier said teasingly while Bailey buried her head in his chest, "but remember, you're invited guests. Don't try to stay all night. This is, after all, our anniversary, and I want to celebrate it personally with my wife."

As everyone was coming in, Xavier excused himself. "I'm going to take a shower," he whispered to Bailey and took the back staircase to the second floor.

By the time he returned to the first floor, the party was in full swing. The music was playing, the glasses of wine had been poured, and everyone had a plate in their hands. The entertainment started with watching the wedding DVD and looking through the wedding albums. After that, the women gathered in the kitchen so they could have some of Bailey's ginger tea and a little girl talk.

It was after midnight by the time the anniversary couple finally got into bed. "You know, Bailey, I did enjoy that surprise. Although I didn't realize we were already six months into the marriage. So thank you for the celebration. Also, I do actually have something for you." He pulled her close and, just before he kissed her, he asked, "Are we going to celebrate every six months?"

She pushed away from his intoxicating closeness. "Just for the first year. Why?"

"Well, my memory is not that good, and besides that, it could get very expensive for me."

"What do you mean expensive?" she asked, perplexed. "We don't have to have prime rib every anniversary."

"No, that's not what I mean. I may not be able to afford a gift every six months."

"Xavier, you didn't give me a gift, did you? You said you didn't remember it had been six months."

"Honestly, I didn't, but when Victor called me earlier this week and asked what time the party was getting started, I thought you deserved a surprise. Reach under your pillows and tell me what you think."

Bailey sat up and turned on the bedside lamp. She got out of bed, picked up her pillows, and found a long black velvet flip-top box. With shaking hands, she lifted the top and revealed a diamond and emerald double-strand tennis bracelet with matching diamond and emerald stud earrings.

She didn't say anything; she just stood beside the bed looking at the jewelry in the box. Xavier got out of bed and walked around it to stand behind her. "Do you like it?" he asked.

She turned to face him. "This is the most wonderful thing that anyone has ever given me. It's so beautiful, it's…magnificent." She was at a loss for words. "Where and when would I ever wear these?"

"How about right now, in this room? Put them on. Let's see how they look on you."

It was a pleasantly long night for Xavier and Bailey. So much so that it was almost noon before they both woke up.

"Good afternoon, Mr. Monroe, would you like to place an order for brunch?" Bailey asked when they woke.

"Right now, I'm not hungry for food," he said. "Come here." He pulled her toward his already excited body and kissed her deeply, for starters.

Chapter 29: He's a Good Man

The women of the Monroe family were close-knit, and they took every opportunity to get together. The third Saturday of the month became the time when they would gather at each other's houses and have a "hen party." This month, it was being held at Olivia's, and it just so happened that this hen party was held the day after the half-year wedding anniversary celebration. Everyone was still in high spirits. The ladies were in the kitchen finishing the cleanup, and it seemed that this month's topic of discussion was Bailey, the newlywed.

"So, what did your husband give you for your anniversary?" Victoria asked Bailey.

"How do you know I got a gift?" Bailey asked.

"Girl, men gossip more than women," Kendra answered. "We all know because Clayton sold it to him, of course."

"Stop stalling and tell us what you got," Olivia prodded.

When Bailey told them, the comments flooded in.

"Oh, clearly you're still in the honeymoon stage."

"That's nice."

"Enjoy it while it lasts."

Then Helen Monroe injected, "You can probably expect things

like that for about five years, Bailey, and then they become convinced you're staying, and all the niceties go away. By then, they can't even remember to put down the toilet seat."

Everyone laughed, and then Victoria got a little more personal. "So, Bailey, it's been six months and you never told us. How was that wedding night?"

Bailey looked surprised. "Stay out of my affairs and mind your own business, Victoria."

"Bailey," Olivia said, "it's a tradition in this family that the newest sister shares her special night with the others."

After being assured it was just between them, Bailey shared. "Well, as you all know, there was a situation not six hours after we were married. And when the brothers came, I went to our bedroom and cried myself to sleep. After a while, I felt Xavier's weight on the bed. He laid down, folded me in his arms, and we slept that way all night."

Bailey looked around the room and saw the sympathetic looks. She continued. "The next morning, while we were having tea, we talked about the situation, and he promised me that as long as we were together, I had nothing to worry about because he would protect me and keep me safe."

"Yeah, yeah," Kendra said, "love, honor, protect all in the marriage vows. Cut to the chase, give us details, girl." Then, in a stage whisper, she asked, "Did he live up to his reputation? Is he, you know…the wild stallion?"

Bailey continued as though Kendra had not said anything. A tear gently rolled down her cheek before she continued. "Later that night, after the family meeting, he taught me how to make love. He didn't even mind that it was my first time. Afterward, we took a bubble bath together, and he soothed me while assuring me that the next time we made love, it would be more enjoyable for me."

Bertha stood and handed her daughter a tissue. "I knew he was a good man, baby girl," she said and hugged her daughter.

Olivia, trying to lighten the mood, slid off the kitchen stool and slowly walked across the kitchen to Bailey. She took her hand and said, "Girl, are you telling us that you were a virgin up until you got married? How the heck did you do that?"

Bailey looked at her sister-in-law with sad amusement. "Have you met my mother?"

Chapter 30: Getting Friendly

Making friends was not easy for Bailey. She was not an open person. She rarely reached out to strangers. So when Marie Jackson returned to work, Bailey reminded herself of the request she had made to her boss.

"Good morning, Miss Jackson, welcome back," she forced herself to say.

When Marie made no indication that she'd even heard her, Bailey knew this was going to be an arduous undertaking.

Bailey followed the attorney into her office and continued. "This is your schedule for the week, and these are the materials you will need to get started today. Let me know what I can do to help you."

As Bailey was leaving the room and reaching for the doorknob to close the door, Marie invited her back into the office. "Mrs. Monroe," she said, "Bailey, wait. Come in and have a seat, please."

Bailey was surprised but complied with the request.

"I understand that you asked my brother not to fire me," Marie said. "Why did you do that after the way I've treated you?"

"Miss Jackson, good jobs are difficult to find in this day and time, and even though you are a good attorney, if you have a resignation or a termination on your résumé, it will be difficult for you to get rehired. I wouldn't want that for anyone. Besides, I don't make friends very easily, but I think we should try to be friends if that's alright with you."

"Call me Marie. I need to ask you if you would forgive me for my rude behavior and my hurtful words. I've never had a friend before, but I would like to be your friend."

The ladies stood, and before Bailey left the office, they hugged. Closing the door, Marie walked into her brother's office and tearfully thanked him for not firing her.

"And you were right," she said, "she is a nice person. I think that we can be friends."

It seemed as if the atmosphere of the office changed that day. Several days after Marie's return, Ja'Nell asked, "Miss Bailey, have you noticed how nice Ms. Jackson is now?"

"She's a nice person, Ja'Nell. We had lunch together this afternoon, and we had a really good time. You should come next time."

Marie was one of Bailey's two friends outside of the Monroe clan. She felt that Marie was someone she could have a lasting relationship with. Even Marie's brother was pleased with the change in his sister's attitude.

"Bailey Anderson-Monroe, you are a miracle worker," he told her. "My sister seems to have had a change of heart. She's lost her scowl, and she appears to be a little more open-minded and friendly. So, whatever you did, don't stop." Before he walked away, he added, "Melody and I enjoyed ourselves at the anniversary party. Thanks for inviting us."

Chapter 31: Taking Measures

Xavier was upset, mostly with himself, and he chastised himself during the commute to and from work that Monday. *I can't believe that I got caught up in that trap*, he thought. *I acted like a love-sick puppy the whole damned weekend.*

His thoughts were intense and powerful. He was angry with himself; he couldn't believe that he had actually purchased a gift for her to celebrate six months of marriage. However, he had to admit that the bracelet and earrings looked really good on Bailey, especially since she'd had nothing else on at the time.

It was not and never had been his intention to get drawn into the "husband" mindset. *I've got to stay away from her as much as possible. She's a seductive, cunning, and scheming woman.*

Xavier had almost convinced himself that he was just beginning to see through that innocent act she used to get him so caught up in the relationship. Throughout the day, his feelings kept wavering. On the one hand, he knew Bailey was not totally responsible for how he was feeling and acting. On the other hand, he had to admit she was one of the most open and honest people he knew.

And still, on the other hand, she does seem to be able to mesmerize me with her charms. That little "innocent" act of hers could wear anyone down. She catches me off guard and snakes her way through my defenses. She gets my mind so twisted I can't seem to think straight. She's trying to get me caught up in some kind of permanent relationship. Well, have I got news for her!

Xavier took a deep breath and wished he could resist Bailey.

I never meant for anything like this to happen. What's wrong with me? I never intended for this situation to get so out of control.

He was in an extremely disagreeable mood by the time he arrived home. When Bailey met him at the door and asked him about his day, he told her he didn't feel well and was going to take a shower and go to bed early. When she offered him a kiss, he pushed her aside. "I don't feel like all of that tonight."

"Okay," she said. "I can tell that you really are tired." As she walked into the kitchen, she asked, "Do you want dinner in bed?"

"No! I just want to be alone. Can you do that? Can you just leave me alone? I don't want anything from anybody! I especially don't want you in my face tonight. Could you just…" He walked away, leaving her standing in the middle of the room with tears in her eyes, stunned and wondering what had just happened.

That night, she ate dinner alone, but she was too upset to eat much. Bailey decided it was best for the situation if she slept in the guest room near the main staircase, especially since the door to the master bedroom was locked.

I know that his job is strenuous, and I have to accept the fact that sometimes he's going to come home with some frustrations and even some disappointments. I also know he didn't mean to but he hurt my feelings, she thought.

She sat up in the guest bed for most of the night with a box of tissues until she fell asleep from exhaustion. By the time she woke on Wednesday morning, Xavier had already left for work.

By seven o'clock that night, Xavier had ignored six calls from Bailey and had not bothered to listen to her messages. He decided to get himself a hotel room for the rest of the week and think things through. Then he would go home for the weekend and deal with the situation.

When he wasn't focused on his work, Xavier mentally reviewed the events of the previous weekend. *I really can't believe that I fell for her tricks and schemes*, he thought to himself. *She's been pulling me around by the nose for six months. I can't believe her, using that innocent act, cooking that "special meal," showing the wedding video, looking through the photo album. Acting like this is a real marriage. As a matter of fact, she's acting like we're a loving couple. I don't think I can make it through two years of this. Man, what have you done to yourself?*

Bailey was confused about Xavier's behavior. She kept going over the events of the weekend and the past several days, but she couldn't think of anything that had happened that would justify his anger.

Finally, she decided that if her husband didn't come home tonight, she was going to have Ja'Nell drop her off late tomorrow morning at the station. She was going to take the train to the city, go to his office, and ask him to lunch so they could talk.

After he checked into the hotel and had his bags taken to his room, Xavier went to the hotel restaurant to dine and read over the transcript of a conviction that was being appealed. After he placed his order with the waiter, a shadow fell over the table.

"Hello, Skippy. I see that you are eating alone. Do you want some company?"

Things are going from bad to worse, he thought. *Great. This is all I need.*

"Hello, Priscilla," he said. "Why are you here? What do you want?"

She sat down even though he had not invited her to do so. "Skippy, I've tried to contact you several times, and you haven't answered any of my letters. I really want us to be friends again."

"Priscilla, as you know, I've moved on. I'm married now.

There's no room in my life for a relationship between you and me, not now or in the future," Xavier said, looking down at the information in the open folder before him.

"I know that you can't possibly mean any of that. You couldn't be happily married, not to her, anyway. She's not even your type. Don't you remember? You and me? We were so right together. I need you to forgive me for the way I left you. Back then I was young and scared, but I'm more grown up now. I've thought it over, and I know that it was wrong of me to leave like I did. I should have married you. We had something special. I still love you. You should surely still know that. And I believe that you still love me, too. Can we start over again?"

Priscilla was leaning across the table as Xavier slowly and deliberately closed the folder and slid it into his briefcase. Then he turned and looked directly at his former fiancée. Without so much as a blink, he said, "You did me a favor all those years ago. Back then, I wasn't ready to be married. Your leaving gave me the opportunity to think straight and decide that instead of wasting my time chasing the opposite sex, I needed to focus and concentrate on honing my craft."

Xavier sat back and offered his tablemate a slight smile. "So now when I look back at what happened then, I consider your betrayal an act of extreme generosity because it helped me learn how to focus on what's important in life, and that's being the best attorney I can be. At this point, there's no room in my life…in me and my wife's life…for you."

Not wanting to believe what Xavier was saying and hating even more the finality in his voice, Priscilla moved her chair closer to him. "Are you happy, Skippy? Is it really that easy for you to move on with your life without me being a part of it? We had something good, you know, and I think it can be good again."

"Priscilla," he said, "it's over. I've moved on, you should do the same."

She reached for his hand across the table. "You don't mean that, Xavier, I know you don't."

Pulling his hand away, Xavier stood slowly so as not to draw any undue attention to what was happening between him and Priscilla. "What we had is over. Let's not do this again. Have a good evening, Priscilla."

With a pout on her face, Priscilla Grayson stood quickly. "You don't mean that, Skippy. You can't. You promised me that we would always be together."

"That was part of our childhood fantasy, Priscilla. We're both grownups now. Goodbye." With that said, Xavier took his seat again, pulled the folder back out of his briefcase, opened it, and resumed reading.

As she walked away, Priscilla whispered to herself, "If you think this is over, Skippy, then you are mistaken. You were mine once, and you'll be mine again."

Chapter 32: Let's Talk

Bailey arrived at the Hyatt Place and went to the check-in desk. "Oh, good afternoon, Mrs. Monroe," the desk clerk said. "Your husband didn't say that you were coming. Would you like the key to the suite now?"

"No," she said, "thank you. But could you have my bag taken to the room, please?"

Bailey had called ahead and gotten an appointment with Xavier through his secretary. As a result, when she walked into his office and saw that his appointment was with Bailey, he didn't bother to stand but just looked at her with a scowl on his face. "What are you doing here? This is not a good time. Just turn around, go home, and we can talk there."

"How are we going to do that, Xavier? You haven't been home all week. All I need to know is what did I do? What happened that has prompted you to treat me like an enemy and stay away from home?"

She looked so despondent standing across the desk from him. He could hardly keep his seat, but he had to. He couldn't get pulled in again. "Bailey, there is no problem. You haven't done anything. We have a backlog of work to clear up, and if I stay here, I can get it done sooner and get home by the weekend. Now, would you please leave so I can get back to work?"

Seeing her facial expression change from hope to despair almost melted his resolve, but he wasn't going to let her get to him—not again. He looked down at the papers on his desk and didn't look up again until he heard his office door softly close.

Walking out of Xavier's office was a brutally wounding undertaking for Bailey. His callous indifference hurt her deeply. Bailey never thought she would ever be subjected to the detached and insensitive treatment that Xavier was known to use in the courtroom.

She had known that they would not be able to solve the problem then and there, but she was hoping he would at least act like he was pleased to see her. She felt dejected, disheartened, and genuinely hurt by his cold, heartless treatment.

As she was slowly making her way back to the hotel, Bailey tried to decide what to do. She thought she could retrieve her bag from the room and get on the next train, or she could go to another hotel, get a room, and leave in the morning. Or she could go to the Hyatt, wait for him, and have a heart-to-heart before she left. One thing was for sure: When she got back to the room, the first thing she was going to do was have a good cry.

Even if Xavier wanted to go home tonight, he couldn't. The last commuter left at 8 p.m. It was now 8:30, and he was just leaving the office. Besides, he was so tired he just wanted to get into bed, and the closest bed was at the hotel.

Hyatt, here I come, he thought to himself as he left the justice building. He was getting out of the taxi in front of the hotel when a figure stepped out of the shadows and moved toward him.

It was Priscilla. "Are you hungry?" she asked. "I certainly am, and I've been waiting to have dinner with you again tonight."

"Priscilla, this is not a good time. I have a lot of work to do tonight. Besides, I've already eaten," he lied, "and we've already said our final goodbyes. So good night."

Instead of leaving, she stepped close and attempted to embrace him "There you go again, throwing up that wall of resistance. I know you don't mean it."

Just as Xavier leaned back and used his arm to move her away from him, the hotel security guard walked outside. "Is there a problem here? Are you alright, Mr. Monroe? Do you want me to call the cops?"

"No, thank you, Mr. Ward," Xavier said. "The lady is an old friend. She was just leaving." Without a second glance at Priscilla, Xavier walked into the hotel and into an elevator.

The elevator operator smiled and greeted him. "Evening, Mr. DA. How you doing tonight, sir? Bet you're real glad your wife came to see you."

"My wife?" he echoed.

"Yeah, I let her into your suite just a coupla hours ago. She's real pretty. You sure are a lucky man, Mr. DA."

Xavier exited the elevator on the seventh floor and swiftly walked to his suite. When he opened the door, Bailey was lying on the sofa. She opened her eyes and then quickly threw off the blanket and stood.

"I'm sorry," she said. "I had planned on being gone by now, but I guess I fell asleep. Don't worry. I'll leave right now. I didn't even unpack. Maybe I'll see you at home tomorrow night."

Xavier stepped back to block the door. "You're here now, so you may as well stay. Besides, the last commuter left about an hour ago. Let's go get some dinner, and then we can come back here and talk."

"No, thank you," she said, "I'm not hungry."

Chapter 33: Mistaken

They stood looking at each other. He looked at her and saw that her eyes were puffy. He felt a stab of anguish but had to keep his resolve or he would lose his ability to think straight and keep her from getting past his defenses. If not, he could lose his self-control and easily fall under her spell again.

Bailey finally spoke. "What have I done so wrong that it has all of a sudden turned you against me, Xavier? For six months, we have been happy. At least I have been, and I thought you were, too. So what have I done that has caused you to act so pigheaded that you don't even want to be around me?"

Xavier put his hands in his pockets. Bailey looked so forlorn that he wanted to hold her tight and soothe her until the sadness in her eyes went away. But instead of doing that, he walked to the picture window that looked out over many of the city's rooftops.

"You haven't done anything, not directly. It's just that when we are together, I lose all my self-control. Every night I walk into that house and I'm no longer myself, I can't seem to think rationally in my own home. And you. You are a seductive, persuasive, and enticing woman, and I can't seem to resist you. I lose all ability to be free thinking and uninhibited when I'm around you."

He walked away from the window and sat down in the overstuffed armchair. "This marriage was never meant to be genuinely intimate, yet we have been so warm and friendly with each other so often that it's hard to remember this is a contractual relationship. We're actually acting like it's a real marriage. And we both know that it's not. In eighteen months, this charade is going to be over, and we're going our separate ways."

Finally, he had voiced what was on his mind, but it didn't seem to make him feel better. Bailey pulled in a deep breath, folded her arms across her abdomen, and sat down on the sofa. She looked at him warily. "So, all of a sudden it's become an inconvenience for you to be married. Is that it?" Without allowing him to answer the question, Bailey continued. "In the beginning, it was all about how being married would be a contributing factor to your getting this position. Now that you have it, I guess there's no reason to keep me around anymore. Isn't that right?"

She unfolded her arms and took another deep breath.

"You know what, Xavier Monroe, Mr. District Attorney, if you want to terminate the contract, it's alright by me. Just bring me the order of dissolution, and I'll sign it right away. Then you can be free again."

Xavier's face became hard and set. He grabbed the arms of the chair, vaulted from his seat, and grasped her by her arms. "That's not what I'm saying," he said forcefully. "Don't put words in my mouth. We have a signed contract that states we'll be together for two years, and I intend to hold you to it."

Bailey stepped away from him, pulling her arm from his grip. It wasn't until then that he realized he had taken hold of her. He was immediately sorry. For the first time since he had known Bailey, he could see fear in her eyes, and that was not his intent. He quickly put his hands back into his pockets.

"Okay, so you want to hold me to the terms of that contract?" Bailey said to him. "Do you have the same restrictions, or are you operating from a different set of guidelines? Am I supposed to be the housekeeper, your cook, the convenient bedroom entertainment, the listening ear, your social companion, and then disappear until you get hungry or want to satisfy your manly needs again?"

She stood looking at him with a sad and wounded expression on her face, rubbing her upper arms. Then she turned away from him, walked into the bedroom, and picked up her overnight bag.

"You know what, Mr. Xavier Monroe?" she said over her shoulder. "You can do whatever you want. It's probably very difficult for you to be married *and* to be faithful for two years, anyway. I'm leaving. I can't stand to look at you right now. You make me sick!"

"Where do you think you're going?" he demanded as he stormed behind her. "I told you the last train has already left."

"Don't worry about where I'm going. You don't want me in your face. Right? So I'll meet you at your house tomorrow. Oh, yes, and you won't have to worry about locking your bedroom door anymore. I'll stay in the room farthest from you. We can be in the same house for the rest of the contract, but we don't ever have to be in the same room at the same time."

She rolled her eyes then sucked her teeth and pursed her lips.

"You hurt me. You said some things that were uncalled for. You treated me like I had done something terrible to you. What did I do to deserve that? If you're tired of me and don't want to be married to me anymore, then so be it. I'll leave."

Bailey went to the bed to pick up her overnight bag. As she was turning to walk out of the bedroom and make her way to the front door of the suite, she ran into Xavier's hard body. He had been standing behind her. When she walked into him, he touched her arms to steady her. She immediately shrugged his hands away. She hadn't meant to, but when she felt his touch, she gasped and stepped back.

Xavier saw her reaction. Inhaling and pressing his lips together he leaned forward and effortlessly relieved her of the overnight bag, tossing it back onto the bed. Taking in another deep breath, he exhaled slowly, "Just wait a minute, Bailey. If I said and did anything that hurt you, then I'm sorry. But you need to settle down and stop jumping to conclusions."

"Stop jumping to conclusions? What am I supposed to think when you say the things you've said to me and stay away from your own house just so I won't be in your face? I do believe that I've served my purpose with you, and your actions have shown me that it's time for me to go."

He sat down heavily on the bed and looked up at his wife. "Bailey, I'm not good with relationships. When Priscilla left, I shut down completely. I started working day and night to get established in the judiciary field. I promised myself that I wouldn't get sidetracked by anyone or anything anymore. Then here you come being amiable, seductive, and alluring, and you take my mind off my work. All I can think about on that train every night is you! I take the express so I can get to you faster. In the meantime, I find myself growing impatient because the train isn't moving fast enough."

He reached out for her hands and saw her flinch. That little movement gave him pause. It hurt him to see that she was afraid of him. He looked at her arm and saw the remains of the unconsciously aggressive contact he'd had with her a few moments ago.

Taking her hands gently, Xavier continued. "When I get into the car, I begin to ask myself the same questions every night. How is she going to look? What is she going to smell like? I even wonder what delicious meal you've cooked. I've tried to convince myself that you're a witch who has cast a spell on me, but I know that it's simply a case of you having spoiled me, and I like it."

She stood looking down at him as he held her trembling hands. "Xavier, I have never been in a relationship before this one, and you know that. I just never thought I was wife material. Then when we got married and I came to live in your house, I realized that I liked cooking and cleaning for someone else. I liked having someone to talk to. I liked sharing a bed with another warm body. I liked getting the attention, and I appreciated the fact that you did nice things for me. But if you can't handle us being together anymore, I'll just leave."

She snatched her hands from his and ran into the bathroom. Xavier quickly jumped to his feet to follow her, but before he could get to the door, she had closed and locked it. He could hear her sobs through the door.

Rattling the doorknob, Xavier said, "Bailey, come out of there. Don't you do anything silly, we're not finished talking." When she didn't open the door, he said, "I'm going to call maintenance if you don't open this door, do you hear me?" His voice was rising, and he banged his fist on the door. "Woman, open this door, now!"

He heard the lock disengage, and the door opened a sliver. Tearfully, Bailey said, "Don't flatter yourself, *man*. I'm not going to do anything to hurt myself. My world is not going to end because you don't want me. We will just go our separate ways earlier than planned. Now if you don't mind, I'm going to get ready for bed. Don't worry, I won't be trying to entice you and rob you of your precious masculinity. I'll sleep in the living room. I don't want to be in your way."

When she tried to close the door, he forced it open wider and seized her securely, by the arm again, but this time with less pressure. "I told you to stop trying to put words in my mouth. I didn't say I don't want you anymore."

"You did say that. If not directly, it was insinuated. Anyway, it was fun for me while it lasted. Thanks for the memories."

She tried to pull her arm from his grasp and close the door, but he had wedged his shoulder between the door and the frame, and she couldn't break his grip or push him out of the way.

Bailey looked at his hand on her arm and said in a shaky voice, "Would you please let me go, you're hurting me!"

He pushed the door open, gently pulled her through the doorway, and surrounded her with his arms. Breathing heavily and in a voice that was almost a whisper, he said, "I'm sorry. I didn't mean to hurt you." He kissed the top of her head and held her to his chest. "I don't know what we are arguing about, but I want to call a truce. Maybe we can talk in the morning. Right now, I'm really tired and I want to get some rest. But I want you next to me while I'm sleeping."

Slowly, Bailey's arms moved around Xavier's waist. His arms pulled her closer, and he tenderly rubbed her back. They stood in their embrace for several minutes until her breathing slowed and his heart rate returned to normal.

Later, they showered and prepared for bed. When she stepped out of the bathroom, he took her hand, led her to the armchair in the living room area, and sat down with her on his lap. He felt like such a heel when her silent tears began falling, wetting his T-shirt. He realized he had just broken his promise of protection to her.

Neither one had anything else to say. They just sat cuddled in the chair until she fell asleep. Then he carried her to the bed and laid down beside her. Taking one last look at her, he could still see the faint tear tracks on her cheeks. He kissed each cheek, turned off the lamp, and went to sleep.

Chapter 34: Getting Past the Honeymoon Stage

Bailey woke to find Xavier watching her. "What's wrong?" she asked with her hand over her mouth.

He smiled. "Nothing, I just like to watch you sleep."

She covered her face. "Well, stop. I look like a mess in the morning. I don't have on any makeup, my hair is not combed, and I haven't brushed my teeth."

"You look like a Nubian queen to me," Xavier said as he reached across the bed and caressed her face. Then he gave her a sincere look. "Bailey, I don't know what last night was all about. I don't even know what the last few days have been about, but I want to apologize to you for my behavior."

She looked into his eyes and offered him a slow smile. "You know what, Mr. District Attorney, you're so cute in the morning that I don't think I could harbor any feelings of resentment. But I just need to know for myself what that was all about."

"Well, let's just try to figure it out tonight," he said. "Stay in town today, and we'll go home together."

"I don't know what I would do all day. But I guess I can find the nearest department store and maybe we can have lunch together, what do you think?"

He got out of bed and tucked the bedding around her. "You can start by staying in bed for a little while longer. I can't have lunch with you, but just in case you do find that store, here's a little something to help get a sexy silky thing you can wear tonight for *my* eyes only."

He put his debit card on the nightstand.

"The pin number is 38-29," he said with a wink. Then he added, "They're your measurements. Every time I use it, I'm reminded of you." He climbed back into bed, and it was much later when they went in to take a shower.

She returned to the bed, piled the pillows behind her, and turned on the television. After he left, she dozed off and on until she was sure the stores were open. Then she set out to find that *sexy silky thing* that might intrigue him.

Chapter 35: Home Again, Together

"It feels good to be home," Xavier said as he drove the car into the garage. "I can't wait to see that little something you got for me today."

Just when he deactivated the house alarm, Xavier's cell phone rang. Looking at the screen, he frowned. "Agent Wilson. Yes, I am at home. Yes. She is right here with me. Okay. Thank you."

When he hung up, Xavier led Bailey into the house. He secured the garage doors, as well as the door from the garage to the mudroom, and then he closed and locked the door from the mudroom to the kitchen. He walked through the kitchen into the entry hall, checked the front door, and then went to the dining room to make sure that the security bar was in place on the sliding glass doors. After all of that, he reset the perimeter alarm and finally returned to the kitchen, where he turned off the lights.

He walked over to Bailey, who was standing in the middle of the kitchen, and said matter-of-factly, "Let's go into the den and watch a little television for a while." He touched her back, and they headed toward the den.

"What's going on?" she asked him. "Who was that on your phone? Why should we go into the den?"

Because he could feel her getting tense, he decided to tell her the truth. "I've been working on a convictions appeal, and the prisoner has escaped. Because he has promised to kill the judge and everyone involved in the case, we have been put on alert. Now, let's go into the den. It's in the middle of the house. There are no large windows or other exits, and the state police and the FBI feel it's the safest, most self-contained place to be while in the house. Don't worry, we're safe. There are two agents. Actually, four if you count their K-9s posted outside."

In the den, Xavier checked the bathroom, looked in the linen closet, and locked himself and his wife in the room. The next thing Xavier did at first surprised Bailey, then frightened her. He crossed the room, sat at his desk, and unlocked and opened a drawer. He reached in, and when he lifted his hand, he was holding a gun. Bailey watched as he checked the clip and loaded the gun. Then he secured the safety lock. Finally, he took out his phone and sent a text message.

During all of that time, Bailey stood in the middle of that room watching him. When he turned around to look at her, he had a smile on his face that didn't touch his eyes. "We have to stay here until we get the all-clear from the law enforcement agencies. We may be here for a while."

Seeing the ashen pallor on her face, Xavier holstered the firearm and stood in front of Bailey. "From this night forward, I'm never going to argue with you again about that stash of junk food in the linen closet or challenge you about this little refrigerator taking up valuable space. Since we're going to be here a while, we can at least sustain ourselves. We have lots to eat and drink. There's also the television and the stereo for entertainment. We even have sleeping arrangements, and the most important thing, we have lavatory facilities. We could live in this room for a good while."

Xavier tried speaking softly to put her at ease. When he embraced her, she was trembling, and a look of fear brimmed in her eyes. "Why do you have a gun?" Bailey asked. "When did you get it? Is that gun necessary? How long are we going to have to be locked up in this room?"

"I've had this gun and the permit to carry for a year. The governor and lieutenant governor are also armed. The chief of police believes it's necessary because of situations like this." He pulled her closer. "We are going to be here for however long it takes. But I'm going to be here with you the entire time. Like I promised, I'm not going to let anything or anybody harm you."

As he led her across the room and away from the desk, he smiled and said, "Come here, girl, let's get our minds on something more pleasant. What's in the bag?"

When she looked down, she saw she was still holding the overnight bag in one hand and the department store bag in the other. She let him take them from her and then allowed him to return her to his embrace. They held their embrace for several minutes until he felt her body relax. Then he pulled her onto the sofa and into his lap.

"Let's see what's on the late show," he said.

While being together like this could not be considered lots of fun, they used the time to finish the discussion that was started at the hotel. "So, Mr. Monroe," Bailey said, "you still contend that you have relationship issues, and therefore the incidents of the past week are a result of your disability?"

They were sitting on the freshly made-up mattress of the sofa bed that they had opened. Between them were several bottles of apple juice and water, a bag of pretzels, and some string cheese.

"Yes," he replied, "that is my contention, madam. So what do you say? Do you forgive me?" He tried to make a sad face.

"Oh, no, you don't get off that easy!" Bailey said, trying to maintain a somber look. "Do you know that you hurt my feelings when you told me you just wanted to be left alone? Then you forced me to sleep in the guest room where I cried myself to sleep, and then you left me without saying goodbye. You were mean to me, and I'm still mad at you about it!"

"Well, let me make it up to you. It was never my intention to hurt you. I was just confused and scared."

"Scared and confused about what? What is there to be scared about?"

He closed the space between them, stretched out across her lap, and looked into her eyes. "I'm stepping out onto an emotional limb in this relationship, and when I do things spontaneously, it leaves me feeling exposed and vulnerable. Those are feelings that I have never had to approach before."

"Are you expecting me to excuse your actions?" she asked, looking down into his incredibly handsome face.

"Yes, yes I do. But most of all, I want us to have some amazing makeup sex."

"Oh, no, you don't. You are not getting off that easy. You owe me."

"I'm trying to make up for it right now, woman."

They both laughed as he pulled her down for a kiss.

At 1:50 a.m. Sunday morning, Xavier's phone rang. He didn't touch it right away. When it rang again, he looked at the screen, picked it up, accepted the call, listened, and repeated a series of numbers. Finally, he disconnected.

When he looked at Bailey, he could see her eyes open in the dim glow of the night-light. "You stay here. Lock this door when I go out, then go into the bathroom and close that door, too." He took the gun from the table beside the bed, unlocked the door, and slid out of the den into the entry hall.

After what seemed like an eternity but was actually thirty minutes, Xavier unlocked the door to the den and returned the gun to its place. Then he knocked on the bathroom door and stepped inside.

"Bailey, sweetheart, it's over," he said. "You can come out now."

When she slid back the curtain and stepped out of the tub, he offered her a robe. In the living room, she was introduced to FBI agent Wilson and chief of the state police, Bradley Preston. The men greeted her with a nod and a smile.

"Mrs. Monroe, we're sorry for the inconvenience of the last few hours," Agent Wilson said, "but things are satisfactory now."

With that, both gentlemen shook Xavier's' hand and left.

Chapter 36: First Year is Bliss?

Over the course of the following six weeks, Bailey had her moments of anxiety. There were times when she would scream and flail in her sleep. But Xavier was there to hold her and comfort her until she was at ease again. Xavier was also tense and on edge, and when he was, Bailey gave him space until he settled down and came looking for her. In the beginning, the couple refused social invitations and preferred to stay home together after work every day and on the weekends. Xavier called it their healing time. Bailey called it their bonding time.

The next hen party was held at their home. That particular Saturday, the men were formally invited too. It was the first time in three months that Xavier and Bailey spent time with anyone else, and everybody had lots of fun. During the "ladies in the kitchen" time, Bailey again seemed to be the topic of discussion.

"What were you and the wild stallion doing while you were locked in the den for a day and a half?" Kendra asked laughingly.

"Leave me alone," Bailey told her sister-in-law. "Here, have something to eat." She offered Kendra the cheese and cracker platter.

Olivia chimed in next. "Really, Bailey, how did you and baby brother get through more than thirty hours in that room?"

"Follow me," Bailey said mischievously as she stood and walked from the dining room into the den. She went to the linen closet and opened the door. "Before that night, Xavier would constantly chide me about how impractical and childish it was of me to stock half of this closet with junk food and to have this little refrigerator in here filled with water, juices, and cheese all the time. Since that weekend, he's been taking inventory and restocking the closet himself."

The ladies laughed as they returned to the dining room. "So how do you feel right now, are you over the situation?" Victoria asked.

Bailey told the ladies how hard it had been for her at night for a little more than a month, and how Xavier would call her every hour when they were apart. "He played the man role of not showing his vulnerable side, but we helped each other get through it. It took a lot of patience on our part, and now it's just a bad memory."

After everything had truly settled down and they were back into an amiable routine, the couple agreed that they needed to take a break from things for a while to help reset their minds and get better acquainted with each other. Xavier also wanted to take some time away to celebrate their first anniversary. In order to justify his suggestion and convince Bailey to accept it, he said, "We never really had a honeymoon, and since I'm due a vacation, let's go to Niagara Falls." Bailey readily took the time off, and they set out on their honeymoon adventure.

Although the tours of the falls from both the Canadian and American sides were nice and the visits to the historic museums were interesting the couple spent much of their time in the hotel suite, entertaining themselves with activities they hadn't taken time to do before now. They told jokes and funny stories to each other.

She was pretty good. He had no talent for telling jokes. Bailey alleged that he had no sense of humor. He regrettably agreed with her.

They shared their fears and vulnerabilities with each other. She was afraid of his temper, and so was he. He was remorseful, and he promised not to let his temper get the best of him again with her.

They each told the other their likes and dislikes. She liked to read and listen to soft music. He liked to have quiet times when he didn't have to talk or interact with others. She disliked arguments. He disliked having his space invaded. Xavier sang to Bailey, a talent she didn't know he had. Bailey sketched a portrait of Xavier. He was impressed with her artistic ability.

They danced to their favorite music; anything slow so they could be close. She liked the lean, muscular feel of his body. He liked the soft, curvy feel of hers. She gave him a massage. His body was taut and well-developed. He combed and brushed her hair. It felt soft, was shiny, and smelled like chamomile and lavender, which were quickly becoming his favorite scents.

She talked about being an only child. He laughed and called her overprotected. He talked about being the youngest child. She laughed and called him a spoiled brat. They read a book together, taking turns reading out loud. His voice was strong and steady. Her voice was soft and mellifluous. By the end of the week, they were rested and almost ready to return home.

"I've had such a wonderful time, I almost hate to go back home," Bailey said as they were packing.

"I feel the same way," he said. "Had I known we were going to have such a good time, I would have tried to get the full two weeks."

"What made you think that it wasn't going to be fun?" She

stepped up to him and looked up into his face. "I'm good company."

He looked down at her. "I know that you're good company, but there's still one thing that I wish I had done."

She frowned. "What was that?"

He stepped back and reached into his pocket. "I wish that I had given you this before now so we could have some incredible thank-you sex." He was beaming as he handed her a small velvet envelope. Inside was a platinum chain, and on it was a single pearl framed on each side by tiny teardrop diamonds. "Happy anniversary, Bailey," he spoke in a low, sexy tone before he kissed her.

Chapter 37: The Best Laid Plans

Priscilla Grayson was used to getting what she wanted, and she wanted Xavier Monroe. Priscilla had determined her game plan, and she set about to put her plan into action.

The first step in her plan was to reacquaint herself with Xavier. One afternoon, she went to his office demanding to see him, but much to Priscilla's dismay, his secretary told her that Mr. Monroe was unavailable.

Not to be deterred, Priscilla's next step was to make an appointment with Xavier, but when she called the justice building, she was once again told that the district attorney was unavailable by the switchboard operator.

Finally, after so many unsuccessful attempts to get to Xavier, she went to her brother and sister-in-law's house. That was when she found out that the Monroes were on a delayed honeymoon celebrating their first anniversary.

Priscilla was experiencing the sting of disappointment as she thought to herself, *I've got to do something.* Pacing the floor of her apartment, she thought, *I don't intend to let them be together too much longer. He's mine, and it's time he knew it.*

On the Sunday after the Niagara Falls trip, the couple attended the church pastored by Caleb Grayson, who was not only Priscilla's brother but also married to Xavier's sister Victoria. The New Metropolitan House of Worship had a large membership that included almost every member of the Monroe family: Judge and Mrs. Monroe, Clayton and Kendra Monroe, Victor and Delores Monroe, and Olivia and Trevor Williams, as well as all of their children.

During the meet and greet portion of the service, Priscilla strolled over to where Xavier and Bailey were standing. While Bailey was two pews away from her husband being greeted by several of the church mothers, Priscilla stood in front of Xavier, turned her back to Bailey, and began touching and stroking his arms and chest.

"Just where have you been, Skippy? I've been trying to get in touch with you for a while now," she pouted at him as he took a step back.

Victoria, seeing the situation, stepped in immediately and shuttled Priscilla away. "What's wrong with you? Are you crazy? My brother is a happily married man. Stop making a spectacle of yourself."

Priscilla pulled away from her sister-in-law and repeated a lie that she had been telling herself. "He's not that happy. If he was, he would not have had dinner with me in Des Moines. It was almost like old times again. He still loves me, and we are going to be together soon," Priscilla said and walked away.

Immediately after the service, Priscilla tried to get to the parking lot before Xavier could leave but was too late. Pointing at the car as it pulled out of the church parking lot, Priscilla said, "That's alright, I know where you live, and I have a plan. We are going to be together soon, just wait and see."

Driving home from church, Xavier gave his wife a quick glance. "You look fantastic today, Bailey. I didn't think the bracelet and earrings would look that good on you fully dressed," he said with a wanton smile. "Don't forget we haven't had that thank-you sex for the anniversary necklace yet, either."

When he reached over and squeezed her knee, Bailey gently slapped his hand. "You behave yourself. You know that we are having our families over for dinner this afternoon."

"Well, they won't be there all night, you know," he said with that smile again.

Chapter 38: The End is Near

After dinner, the men took out the card table and began playing games of checkers, dominoes, and spades. The older children played Scrabble in the dining room; the younger children went to the basement family room to watch videos; and the women went to the kitchen to help with the cleanup.

"So, when should we expect a little Xavier to be running around this house?" Olivia asked.

Immediately, Bailey answered, "Are you crazy? We've been married for a total of twelve months, give or take a few weeks, and you're talking about a baby? Leave me alone, please."

"Actually," Kendra put in, "that's not such an outlandish question. I think the two of you would make wonderful parents. Have you two even talked about having children?"

"No, and I don't think we'll be having that conversation for a long time," Bailey said. "Now, change the subject. All we talk about during these dinners is me and my husband. Let's find another topic."

For the men, it seemed that Xavier was also the necessary topic of their discussion. And to start things going, Clayton pointedly asked, "So, baby brother, how was that dinner with Priscilla?"

Xavier looked at his brother with a deep, scowling expression. "Man, what are you talking about?"

"Stop the innocent act, X," Trevor said. "Priscilla told Victoria in church this morning all about it."

Judge Monroe leaned toward his son. "Are you and Bailey having problems, son? You know the answer is not with another woman. Remember I asked you if you were sure about marrying this girl, and you said yes. What's going on?"

Disdainfully, Xavier replied, "I think Priscilla is stalking me. Every time I look up, she's there. She's shown up at my office. She's been sending me notes. She was even in De Moines when I was given my appointment. She must be talking about the time I spent a week in the city trying to work on a backlog of cases. I was having dinner in the hotel restaurant, and she showed up at my table. I didn't want to make a scene. I told her there was nothing between us anymore and asked her to leave me alone, then she stood and left the restaurant."

"Do you want me to talk to her for you?" Caleb asked.

"No, thanks. I think I better handle it myself."

Now it was Victor's turn to ask questions. "So are you happy, then? How are you and Bailey doing now?"

Looking sharply at his brother, Xavier asked, "Now? What do you mean now?" He was hoping that Victor didn't know anything about the argument he and Bailey had had at the hotel.

"I mean now. Are you two getting to know each other better? Has she started driving you crazy with her list of honey-dos? Has she had any meltdowns like women do?"

Xavier looked at his father, then at his brothers and brothers-in-law. Finally, he said, "She's a wonderful woman and an outstanding wife. She's spoiled me. You know, she meets me at the door every night and dinner is always hot and ready to be served.

Man, she's incredible."

When he said that, all of the men in the room laughed. Judge Monroe said, "Son, you can expect those perks until the babies start coming. Then those bonuses all of a sudden stop. They figure they have you hooked by then, and they don't have to try so hard anymore to keep you. Enjoy it now, son. Time is getting short." All the other men nodded their heads in agreement.

"Okay, everybody, let's get these games finished. You all have got to get out of my house. My wife and I need some alone time," Xavier said with a big smile.

Clayton thumped a domino onto the table and said, "Enjoy that, too, baby brother, because eventually that alone-time thing stops being so free and spontaneous, too."

With that, all the young men laughed at full volume, fist bumping and high-fiving each other, making comments like "You got that right" and "Enjoy it while you can."

Chapter 39: What's Going On

"This looks like another one of those personal notes again, Mr. Monroe, so I didn't open it. And here's the rest of your mail," Xavier's secretary, Mrs. Reynolds, said.

Xavier looked at the small, pink, brocade-embossed envelope and dropped it in the drawer along with the others. *I've got to do something about this,* he thought to himself. Then, when the secretary left the room, he gathered all of the pink embossed envelopes together, secured them with an elastic band, and stashed them in his briefcase. *I'm going to have to have a talk with my wife real soon,* he declared before he began to peruse the information in the stack of folders on his desk.

Just before lunch, a noise like the sound of arguing came from the other side of Xavier's office door. Before he could walk around the desk, the door was thrown open and Priscilla Grayson stood in the doorway.

"I'm so sorry, Mr. Monroe, this woman insisted on speaking with you, and she wouldn't take no for an answer. She refused to set up an appointment and just barged her way in," Mrs. Reynolds said in a stressed tone.

"Don't worry about it," he said wearily, "I'll take care of this."

"Alright, then, Mr. Monroe," she said. "I'll just follow protocol." When he gave her a slight nod, she backed out of the room and closed the door.

"Now, Priscilla," Xavier said and gestured, offering her a seat, "what can I do for you today? You have to be quick. I'm really busy this afternoon."

Priscilla sat down, crossed her long, shapely legs, and smiled. "So you want to act official, do you? Okay, Skippy, we'll play it your way. I have told you that I'm going to pursue you until you divorce that thing you married and come back to me. Haven't you been reading my notes? I love you, and I want to spend the rest of my life with you. I know that you feel the same as I do. You're just trying to be loyal to her, but you and I were meant to be together. How long are you going to drag this out?" She stood and walked to the corner of his desk.

"Priscilla, I don't know why you don't stop this pretense. I've told you that there will never be anything between us again. Stop this outrageous behavior. Stop sending me those ridiculous notes and get on with your life. Frankly, I think you're making a fool of yourself. You should grow up and move on! I certainly have. Now, if you'll excuse me, I have work to do."

When a light tap sounded on the door, Xavier called, "Come in."

Two uniformed state police officers came in. "Mr. Monroe, we understand that you have an intruder."

Xavier looked at Priscilla and said, "Officers, would you escort this lady from the building?"

Each officer took an arm, and as they were ushering Priscille from the room, she said, "I can't believe this. Are you really going to do this to me? I won't forget this, Skippy!"

Later that afternoon, Mrs. Reynolds had filled out an incident report and was now asking her boss to sign it. "I know this is standard procedure, Mrs. R, but I hate to do it. At one time, that lady and I were... Well, we used to be more than close friends."

Mrs. Reynolds said, "You know, Mr. Monroe, I've been here through five district attorneys, and believe me, one day you're going to be more than glad you did this. Now, if you want my advice, go home and tell your wife about it." She smiled warmly, picked up the signed reports, and walked out of the office.

To prepare her, Xavier called Bailey at the Jackson and Monroe offices and asked her to go home directly after work. He added that they had to have a serious conversation.

As usual, she was standing at the door between the mud room and the kitchen when he got home. Again, she looked so good that he couldn't do anything but smile. She was warm and pleasant to him. She took his briefcase and helped him out of his jacket, then kissed him as they walked into the kitchen holding hands.

She didn't speak until they were seated at the kitchen table. "Now, what is so crucial that we have to talk about it right now?"

Xavier reached for his briefcase and retrieved the stack of pink embossed envelopes. He threw them on the table. "These are notes from Priscilla Grayson that have been sent to me at work over the last nine months. Today, she forced her way into my office and demanded that I stop playing games and divorce you so that she and I can finally get married."

When Bailey made no comment, he continued. "Do you remember after the six-month anniversary thing when I stayed in the city? Well, when I was having dinner in the hotel restaurant, she showed up, and after we exchanged a few words, she left. Now she claims we had a dinner date. She's called and come to my office with offers for us to have lunch together, and these notes have been coming more frequently lately. There's got to be at least a dozen of them."

"Looks like you have a problem on your hands, Xavier. What do you plan to do about it?" she asked. "Have you talked to Caleb and Victoria? Maybe they can help you."

"No," he replied, not wanting to tell her that all the men in the family knew about it already. "I haven't said anything to anyone except you, today. I'm going to handle it myself."

Chapter 40: It's Complicated

Once again, life in the Monroe house fell into an amiable routine. Xavier believed that they were working on building a friendship. Bailey enjoyed being a wife, even if it was only temporary. They went to work, spent time with their families, and spent time together during their evenings engaged in small talk. He talked about some of the cases he was working on, about how much he liked his secretary and appreciated her efficiency. She listened and smiled while he talked.

One evening during dinner, Xavier noticed that Bailey looked exhausted. "What's going on at work?" he asked. "You look tired."

She told him she was not feeling well, and that she thought she had the flu. "Everybody at the office has been sick. I think it's my turn now."

"Well, in that case, why don't you go to bed? I'll clean up the kitchen and bring you a heating pad and some tea," he said. "Don't think I didn't notice you didn't eat anything."

Smiling halfheartedly, she stood slowly. "I'm going to take you up on that offer, Mr. Monroe. I'm just not hungry lately. I'll be okay soon."

Two weeks after Bailey's bout with the "flu," Xavier arrived home. Bailey's car wasn't in the garage, and she wasn't waiting for him at the door. When he called her cell phone, he was immediately connected to voicemail.

*   *   *

"Mom, this can't be...it just can't be. I don't know how this happened," Bailey cried.

"Baby, this is part of being married. Why didn't you expect it? You should be happy. Why don't you go home and talk to your husband? You'll see, he'll be so happy."

"Mom, you don't understand. This can't happen! It's not part of the contract."

As soon as she said it, Bailey regretted it.

When her mother asked her what she was talking about, Bailey told her the whole story. "What do you mean by a contract marriage? That's the silliest thing I've ever heard. Why would the two of you do something like that?" Bertha asked.

Bailey explained that it was Xavier's dream to be the district attorney and that she only wanted to help him.

"Girl," Bertha replied, "you are talking utter nonsense. Who are you trying to fool? I've known for a while that you had feelings for that man, and when he came to you with this...proposition, you jumped at it because of how you felt about him from way back when. And now you done gone and gotten yourself in a situation. What are you going to do about it?"

"Nothing," Bailey said. "We've been married for twenty months now, and I'm only about six weeks along. If I don't say anything, we can go through with the dissolution of marriage and he won't have to know."

"Are you insane? This is his baby, and I don't think that he or his family would appreciate not knowing about it. Besides, how are you going to keep pregnancy a secret?" Bertha was livid.

"Mom, let me figure this out. Please don't say anything. Promise me you won't say anything, please, Mother."

Bailey grabbed her mother's hands. She looked so desperate that Bertha couldn't refuse her only child. "Oh, alright. I won't say anything. You know this is against my better judgment. But I'll give you your space. For a while. Don't forget, it's my first grandbaby. I should be happy. I should be bragging to everyone, not being afraid someone will find out."

Chapter 41: He'll Never Know

"Where were you?" Xavier said when Bailey finally got home. "I've been home for over an hour now. There's no dinner, and I'm getting a little hungry." He was sitting in the kitchen, and as she entered the room, he stood and walked over to her.

"Well, I'm just getting in," she said. "I'm sorry."

Before she could say anything else, Xavier leaned in toward her, took her by her upper arms, and said, "Sorry just doesn't do anything for me. I called everywhere looking for you. Alex said that the office closed at its regular time. Ja'Nell said you both pulled out of the parking lot at the same time. I called your cell several times, and each time it went straight to voicemail. I had no idea what was going on. You should have called me. Besides, I'm hungry. What are you going to do about it?"

"Oh, I'm sorry, what was I thinking?" Bailey snapped. "I should have known that you wouldn't be able to open the refrigerator door and take out some of those leftovers. And heaven forbid you had to actually heat some of those leftovers in the microwave all by yourself. You know, I work too, and maybe every once in a while I'd like to have someone fix dinner for me. Did you ever once stop to think about that?"

She snatched her arms from his grasp, stormed up the steps to the second floor, and locked herself in the bathroom. Watching Bailey run up the steps in tears and hearing the slamming of the door made Xavier think about what his brothers and his father had told him all those months ago.

"Well," he said under his breath, "I guess the honeymoon is over. She's starting to act like a wife now." He gave a quick chuckle and added, "But don't worry, buddy. Four more months, and it's all over. You'll be a free man once again."

He leaned back against the counter, folded his arms across his chest, and looked at the steps, frowning.

After an hour, Bailey had taken a bath, cried until she had no more tears left, and was too tired to be mad at Xavier anymore. When she walked into the bedroom, there was a bouquet of pink and lavender mini roses on the dresser and a little teddy bear on her nightstand.

She walked to the dresser and breathed in the scent of the flowers. Then she moved them to her bedside table, picked up the teddy and hugged it to her chest, climbed into bed, and fell asleep.

* * *

Slowly opening her eyes, Bailey looked across the bed. Sitting propped up against his pillows was Xavier. "It's about time you woke up, woman. It's Friday night, and I want to celebrate the end of the week with my wife. Are you feeling better?"

When she nodded, he smiled. "Good, come with me."

He got off the bed, took her by the hand, and led her down the stairs. The kitchen table was set, and there was a delicious aroma in the air.

She allowed herself to be led to the table and sat down while Xavier served her dinner.

"Who fixed this creamy chicken noodle soup and these hard rolls?" she asked between spoonfuls of soup and pieces of crisp, buttery roll.

"Do you like it?" he asked. When she nodded, he laughed. "Well, as much as I'd like to, I can't take credit for it. Your mother gave it to me. I stopped by her house when I went out to get the please-forgive-me gifts, and she said this was your favorite comfort meal and that you especially like to eat it when you're sick, stressed, or simply not yourself."

When Xavier started talking about going to her mother's house, Bailey inhaled deeply. She didn't realize she had been holding her breath until she heard him say the word "sick," and she released the air she had been holding in.

They had dinner together, and she sat while he cleaned up. Then he suggested watching a movie. When they went into the den, the lighting was soft, and the sofa bed was pulled out and covered with a big, fluffy, cozy comforter. They climbed under the comforter, and for most of the night, they watched what he called chick flicks. Later, they read several chapters to each other from one of his favorite novels.

Lying on her soon-to-be ex-husband's chest, Bailey listened to the comforting sound of his heartbeat and felt the rumble of his voice. "Thank you for comforting and consoling me," she said. "And I'm sorry about my attitude earlier."

Xavier rewarded her with poignant touches and arousing kisses. This time, the couple spent an affectionate and tenderly passionate night in their den.

* * *

Mornings became rough for Bailey. She woke up sick to her stomach and at times barely made it to the guest bathroom down the hall before everything came up. It seemed to be a vicious cycle.

Every morning, she awoke with symptoms of morning sickness. She drank some milk and ate a banana and salt-free crackers for breakfast. By lunchtime, she was starved, and all she wanted was a fully loaded baked potato and smothered pork chop. Then she would go home and cook for her husband, trying hard not to let the smell of the food get to her.

While Xavier ate a full meal, she ate only a small salad with lemon juice or a plate of steamed vegetables. Sometimes, she just had a few crackers and a glass of milk. Then she would go to bed and the next morning, it would start all over again.

Trying to keep her secret was getting more and more difficult for Bailey. Xavier was so observant lately. "Why aren't you eating more than that?" he would ask. She would say that the doctor thought she was getting an ulcer, or she would tell him that she'd had a big lunch. Then he would walk up to her, hug her, and swat her on her rear end.

On one particular occasion, Xavier came home from work with a box of candy and a huge bouquet of flowers. As he handed them to her, he pulled her into a full-body embrace, smiling broadly. "I don't know what's happening, Miss Bailey," he said, "but you're looking and feeling rather voluptuous lately, and I like it."

Chapter 42: The Return

Right after dinner one evening, as Xavier and Bailey were cleaning the kitchen, the doorbell rang. Opening the front door, Xavier was surprised to see Clayton and Zane standing in the vestibule. No one moved or said anything for several long seconds.

Zane stepped forward and hugged his younger brother. "Xavier, I want to apologize to you for my inappropriate actions. I know it's been almost two years, but I had to get sober first." He grabbed Xavier's hand, pulled him forward, and hugged him again. "Do you think you can forgive me? Would you at least try, please, Xavier?"

Xavier stepped back, his eyes glistening. "Zane, you look good. Of course I accept your apology. I know it's tough for you to come here and do this, and I appreciate it, big brother." He invited them in and they sat in the living room. "Zane, can you tell me why you objected to my getting married? Why did you say those things about Bailey?"

Zane tried to choose his words carefully. He had been told by Clayton and Victor how much Xavier loved his wife, and he didn't want to offend his little brother any more now than he already had.

"We were so close once, X. We were almost inseparable, if you remember. I took you everywhere with me. Then when you went to school and later opened your practice, I felt like you had abandoned me, but at least we were together once a month at Mom and Dad's house. And several weekends throughout the year with the guys. But then things changed."

Zane looked at Clayton and then back at his youngest brother. "When you announced that you were getting married, I thought that that was it, that I would never see you again. The fog in my brain had me thinking that she was taking you away from me completely. I believed that if I could chase her away and split you guys up, then you and I could get our relationship back to the way it was. The way I thought it was supposed to be."

"Zane," Xavier said, "you're my brother. I've always looked up to you. I hated what that alcohol was doing to you, but you wouldn't listen to anyone, so what happened here that night was the final straw, and we had to give you that ultimatum. Have you forgiven us for that?"

"Baby brother, that was the best thing anyone could have done for me. My family saved my life that day." Zane stood and walked back to the front door. "Ask my sister-in-law if I can come back one day and apologize to her, too."

At that very moment, Bailey walked out of the kitchen into the entry hall. The three men stopped, and Xavier walked to her, slid his arm around her waist, and looked at his brother. "Go ahead."

Zane started by saying, "Hello, Bailey."

She looked at him and then into her husband's face. Xavier tightened his hold on her side and gave her an encouraging wink. "Hello, Zane," she said.

"Bailey, I'm so sorry for the way I've treated you. If you can find it in your heart, I would appreciate your forgiveness."

"Zane, if Xavier has accepted your apology, then who am I not to accept it also?" She walked toward her brother-in-law, kissed him on the cheek, and hugged him. "You are welcome in this house anytime," she assured him.

After congratulating his oldest brother again and saying goodnight to Zane and Clayton, Xavier closed the front door and turned to face Bailey. He placed his arm around her waist and whispered an emotional "thank you" into her ear.

Chapter 43: Quittin' Time

Three weeks before their second anniversary, while Xavier was away at a lawyer's convention, a large envelope was delivered to Bluford Drive by a courier. It was addressed to Mrs. Bailey Anderson-Monroe.

When she opened it, she saw that it was the order for the termination of the marriage. Even though she'd been expecting them, she was still a little taken aback to actually see the papers.

Knowing that he would be returning home in three days, Bailey went into action. She packed some suitcases and loaded them into her car. She signed the papers and left them on the table in the entry hall. Finally, she wrote him a note.

Xavier, I'm sorry you were away when the papers came. I would have liked to say goodbye in person. Regrettably, I couldn't take more of my clothes and other belongings with me, so we will have to set a time when I can come back and get the rest of everything. Thank you. Take care of yourself. Bailey Anderson.

Three days later, when Xavier arrived back home, he could tell something was wrong. The first thing he noticed was the stack of boxes in his garage, and that Bailey's car was not there. Then he noticed that the mudroom and the kitchen looked bare. All of

Bailey's knickknacks were gone, and there were no small appliances or canisters on the counters. The kitchen smelled like it had been scrubbed and sanitized.

He walked through the well-organized, spotless butler's pantry into the dining room and saw that all the feminine touches were gone from there also. The familiar and pleasant scents she had carefully maintained throughout the house were no longer lingering in the air.

When he walked into the entry hall, the plants were not there, and the beautiful bright throw rugs were not in their places either. He stood looking around the first floor. Just the eradication of those few things made the house seem empty and cold.

He looked sadly at the unadorned floor void of the rugs, which Bailey had removed. He noticed the empty walls and tables. Then he saw the papers on the telephone table in the entry hall with several keys resting on top of them.

When he picked up the note and read it, he literally growled and ripped the piece of paper into shreds. He was so angry that he was shaking. He snatched up the phone and punched in some numbers.

"Fred! I thought I asked you to cancel this order for dissolution of marriage. Well obviously, you didn't, because while we were at the convention, the papers were delivered to my house!" He slammed the phone down onto the charger and threw the pieces of paper into the air.

Xavier called Bailey's cell phone but was informed that her service had been discontinued. He ran up to the bedroom and looked in the closet. All of her clothes were gone. When he walked back into the bedroom, he saw a large jewelry box sitting on the bed against the pillows. Bailey's jewelry box. He lifted the lid. Inside, he found a collection of bracelets, earrings, necklaces, and Bailey's wedding rings.

Slamming the top of the box down with considerable force, Xavier snatched up the phone beside the bed and punched in another set of numbers. "Hello, Mrs. Anderson. Is Bailey there?"

"Yes, she is," his mother-in-law answered, "but she says she doesn't want to speak to you. Give her a couple of days, Xavier, then call again. She's upset because the papers were delivered while you were gone. That was a bad move, son." Before he could respond, his mother-in-law disconnected.

What followed was a long, lonely weekend in a cold, empty house that had once been full of beauty and comfort.

I've got to do something, Xavier thought to himself. *I don't want to be without her. I love her.*

The last part of his thought made him smile, and then he said out loud, "Yeah, I do. I love her. I love. That woman."

*   *   *

The backlog of cases was finally coming to an end, and because of that, Xavier couldn't take any time off to contend with his personal problems. He remembered Bailey had once said that his professional obligations should always come first.

So on the Monday following his return from the convention, Xavier repacked his suitcase, engaged a ride-share service to the train station, and for the next three weeks, rather than going home to an empty house each night, he stayed at the hotel and was more tenacious and relentless than usual in his prosecutions.

He tried several times during those three weeks to talk to Bailey, but she wouldn't take his calls. His mother-in-law kept telling him to "give her a little more time."

Xavier completed a press conference and was returning to his office to finalize the exit review forms for the biggest case of his career. He had won. Everyone was excited, and they wanted to celebrate.

While his staff was drinking punch and eating cake, the district attorney was in his office working hard. After signing the last document, he shut down his office, said goodbye to his associates, and walked determinedly out of the justice building. In his mind, it was time to go get his wife back—or at least give it a try.

He was so determined to begin his mission that he hired a car service to take him back to Creston instead of spending another night in the hotel and waiting to take the train home the next morning.

When the car arrived, the driver said, "I understand you have to stop by the Hyatt for your luggage." When Xavier nodded, the driver added, "There's another client who will be riding with you this evening. We hope you don't mind, sir. It was a last-minute call, and I'm the only car going that way this evening."

Xavier assured the driver that he didn't mind. However, when they arrived at the hotel, he realized that the other passenger was Priscilla.

While the luggage was loaded, she climbed into the car with a smile as big as a Cheshire cat. "Hello, Skippy, fancy meeting you here tonight." When Xavier remained silent, not even making a gesture of recognition, she continued. "That was an awesome press conference today. All week, the reporters have been giving updates about how well you've done these past few months in clearing up the backlog of cases for the state. You're quite a district attorney, Skippy. Congratulations."

When she tried to rub his knee, Xavier grabbed her hand and held it firmly. "Priscilla, I don't want you to touch me ever again. Do you understand me?"

She snatched her hand away. "I thought you'd be glad to see

me since that little wife of yours has flown the coop."

Xavier said nothing; he just fixed his eyes on her.

Taking advantage of his silence, Priscilla smirked and said, "Oh, yes, I know. I know all about how she just up and left you while you were at some convention. See, I told you that she wasn't right for you. I told you that she doesn't love you, at least not like I do. Nobody does. Forget her. This is a sign that you and I belong together. She's nothing but a lowlife gold digger, anyway. You don't need her, especially since I'm here for you."

Xavier looked gravely into Priscilla's eyes. "Two years ago, I punched my brother Zane in his mouth when he tried to say something disparaging about my wife, and I'm warning you, Priscilla, I will do the same thing to you if you say one more word about Bailey. As a matter of fact, for the next hour or so, don't say anything to me at all."

Priscilla knew that he meant what he said. The person she was looking at was not the boy she had known from childhood, or the young man she had been a constant companion to through puberty, and not even close to the man she had left standing at the altar. She could see that he was now a grown man in his prime. And he had changed. This person was successful, confident, and well-respected. And it seemed that he had developed a very no-nonsense attitude.

The look on his face frightened her. His eyes were hard and dark, his lips were drawn and set, and his stare was callous and fierce. She sank back into the seat of the limousine and didn't speak or even as much as look directly at him for the rest of the commute.

At home, while the driver was unloading his luggage, Xavier glared at his former fiancée. "Priscilla, I don't like the games that you're playing. The time for you and me has passed. My wife and

HOW

I are very happy. And even if we weren't, *you* don't stand a chance of being with me ever again. I'm asking you to leave me alone, or I will have you arrested for stalking a public official, and you can just imagine how nasty that can become."

Chapter 44: Finding Out

Walking into the cold, bare, empty house struck Xavier like a knife through his heart. He lowered his luggage to the floor in the mud room and slowly walked through the first floor of the sterile, unadorned, vacuous dwelling. Looking around, he finally realized what his mother had meant when she called his house cold, bleak, and impersonal. He missed the feminine touches that Bailey had put all around. He especially missed the lavender scents that she somehow fragranced the air with. Inhaling deeply, he admitted, "Bailey, baby, I miss you so much."

Eventually, Xavier made his way back to the kitchen. Standing in the doorway, he allowed his mind to drift back to the good times that he and Bailey had enjoyed in this room. He recalled watching her move around the kitchen the morning after they were married. He remembered being happy to see her smiling face when he arrived home and she would be standing in the door between the kitchen and the mudroom. He thought about the honeymoon that they had taken less than a year ago, and all the things they did there together.

It seemed that a lot of memories of their time together flashed through his mind. They all reminded him that this house was too big, too cold, and too lonely for a single man.

Picking up his suitcase, Xavier made his way up the back staircase to the master bedroom suite. Everything here, too, was just like she had left it. Everything in its place, and a place for everything. Only now most of those things were his, and hardly anything was hers. Standing in the shower with the water flowing over his body, he couldn't tell what was falling faster—the water or his tears. Lifting his right hand, he pounded on the shower wall.

"I'm not doing this. I'm not going to live my life without her!"

An hour later, he was in his car heading toward his mother-in-law's house. When he arrived, he sat in the driveway for fifteen minutes before he got out of the car, slowly walked to the front door, and rang the bell.

"Hello Mrs. Anderson," he said. "I'd like to speak with Bailey, please?"

Without saying anything, Bertha stepped back and opened the door for him to walk through. "We watched the news every night, Xavier, congratulations," she said. "But Bailey is not here. She's in the hospital. I was just on my way there, you should come with me."

Xavier felt his heart skip a beat. "What's wrong with her?" he asked through a closed throat.

His heart was beating so loud that he almost didn't hear when Bertha said, "I think it's best that you ask her that question. Now come on, man, let's go."

* * *

Forcing himself to put one foot in front of the other, Xavier followed Bertha through the front doors of the hospital and into the elevator, up to the fourth floor. Bertha walked directly to the nurses' station and spoke to the doctor there.

"Hello, Randall," she said.

"Well, hello, Bertha. It's good to see you today." He looked at Xavier and asked, "Who is this? Wait. Don't tell me…is this him?"

Bertha nodded and offered a half-smile. "Yes, this is Bailey's husband."

"I'm going to take that daughter of yours to task," Randall said. "She didn't tell me she was married to the state district attorney. No wonder we haven't seen you since she's been here," he said to Xavier.

"How long has she been here, doctor?" Xavier asked, then added, "Why is she here? What's wrong with her?"

The doctor looked from Xavier to Bertha and back to Xavier again. "You really don't know, do you, young man?" When Xavier shook his head, the doctor looked at him and smiled. "Well, son, as you already know, you are going to be a father. On her last prenatal visit, we discovered that Bailey was dehydrated. We had to admit her to help her out a little. She needed to drastically raise her fluid levels for the wellbeing of the baby, as well as for herself."

In his mind, Xavier asked, *Baby? She's having a baby?*

Then, aloud, he asked, "Is she going to be alright? Is the baby going to be alright? How long has she been here?" Finally, in exasperation, he asked, "Where is she?"

Xavier was shaking. He felt weak, and there was a roaring sound in his ears. He grabbed the corner of the counter for support and leaned against it.

The doctor stepped toward the father-to-be, grasped his arm, led him to a chair, calculated his pulse, and said, "You need to take it easy, son. I want you to sit here for a few minutes." Then, to a nurse, he said, "Get this man some juice, please."

They gave Xavier a bottle of juice and he began taking sips.

"As soon as you feel stronger, you can go see her," Randall said. "She's in room 416, young man. Good luck!" Then he turned to Bertha. "You get to stay with me for a while. Let's go have a cup of coffee."

Xavier stood in the doorway of the hospital room, looking at his wife. She looked so small and defenseless lying in that hospital bed. "Bailey? When is our baby due?" he asked.

When she saw him, tears immediately welled up in her eyes. She didn't answer his question.

"When were you going to tell me that you are pregnant?" Xavier asked as he entered the room.

"This situation was not addressed in the contract. According to the terms of the agreement, our obligations to each other have expired, so telling you about the pregnancy wasn't necessary. If you can remember, I'm back to being *Miss* Bailey Anderson again. And Miss Bailey Anderson doesn't have to report her business to anyone. And that definitely includes you!"

Xavier laughed. "Look at you with that chin pushed out like you mean business. But those eyes still look like a deer caught in the headlights." He stepped further into the room, closer to the bed. "That's my baby, Bailey. You had no right to hide it from me."

The tears spilled from her eyes. "Xavier, you can't have my baby. You don't have time to raise a child. Your job keeps you too busy." She folded her arms protectively over her abdomen. "No. I'm not going to let you have my baby."

Just then, a nurse walked briskly into the room to stop the loud beeping of the machines. "I'm sorry, sir, you have to go. She shouldn't be getting upset like this." The nurse guided him to the door. "Please, sir, you have to go."

Xavier stormed out of the room. He thought, *Where did she get the idea that I was going to take the baby from her?*

At the end of the hall, he saw Helen and Bertha standing together shoulder to shoulder, arms crossed like a united front. They watched him unblinkingly as he walked toward them. "Hello, Mother, when did you get here?"

"Don't hello me, you big lummox," she said and punched him on his shoulder. "How dare you force that wonderful girl into a marriage so you could get your dream job and then drop her like a hot potato now that she's pregnant?" Helen was outraged. "I can't believe you're that selfish! Xavier, how could you?"

With all of that going on, Bertha stepped away. She didn't want to be involved in the conversation between mother and son.

Inhaling deeply, Xavier said, "Okay, Mother. Are you finished? Do you mind if I say something in my own defense? First, let me say that I didn't know she was pregnant. Second, I canceled the order of dissolution with Fred Carrington six months ago, but he didn't follow through, and Bailey got served when I was at the convention. I never meant for that to happen. I don't want to dissolve my marriage." His chest was rising and falling as he took in deep breaths and let them go.

Helen reached up and caressed her son's face. "You love her, don't you?" When he dropped his chin to his chest, she hit him on the arm again. "Well, don't just stand here blubbering to me, go back down there and talk to that girl. She's scared, and she's heartbroken."

When Xavier stepped back through the doorway of room 416, Bertha was standing beside Bailey's bed. He heard Bertha say, "You need to tell him that."

Then he heard Bailey's reply. "No, he doesn't want me, and I'm not going to beg him to stay with me until I have my baby just to have him leave me again."

"I'm not asking you to beg him for anything," Bertha said. "All I'm saying is that you need to communicate with the man. There's a common ground where you both can benefit. You just remember one thing, little girl. He deserves to be part of his child's life, and no matter how you feel right now, that baby deserves a father in its life." Bertha leaned over and kissed her daughter on the cheek then walked past Xavier and left the room.

He walked over to the bed. "I never told you that I didn't want you. And if you knew me as well as you think you do, you would know that I'm not about to stay with anyone I don't love. I'm not going to let you leave this marriage, Bailey Marie Monroe."

He slipped off his shoes, climbed into the bed, and lay next to her. Slowly and gently, he gathered her in his arms.

"I love you. Do you understand? I realized it six months into the marriage, but I wouldn't admit it then. But now I'm ready to admit it to myself and to you. Furthermore, I have no intention of trying to take our child away from you or letting you try to raise our child alone. We are going to do this together, you and me. And maybe he or she will be the first of many."

"We have to get this one here first before we talk about having any more," Bailey spoke through her tears.

She rested on his chest, gathering strength from him. It had been a long four months for her, and during that time she realized, not for the first time, that she loved Xavier Monroe very much. She loved everything about this man. She loved the rumble of his voice in his chest; she loved the sound of his heartbeat; she loved the way he looked; she loved the feel of his arms around her; she loved the way he smelled. But most of all, she loved him.

"Xavier Monroe, I've loved you since that first year we worked together. I never thought you even knew that I existed. You were so detached and indifferent all the time. Then when you needed my help, I was so happy that I would have done anything to be able to spend time with you. So I agreed to marry you, but I never meant to involve you in a situation like this. I don't want you to feel obligated to stay with me just because I'm having a baby."

"This is the last time that I'm going to ask you to stop putting words in my mouth, and most importantly, stop trying to think for me. Instead, I want you to concentrate on getting out of here and coming home to me so that I can take care of you." He kissed her and said, "Both of you."

Chapter 45: Getting Ready

At the home of Judge and Mrs. Monroe, the women gathered in the great room as they usually did when the hen party was held there. Bailey was sitting on the chaise lounge with pillows propped around her.

"How much longer, Bailey?" Victoria asked.

"Three weeks, maybe more, maybe less," Bailey said. "The doctor told me that first babies are unpredictable."

"Bailey, we met a few days ago, and we've built a schedule so that each one of us can be at your house to help you with the baby when Xavier is at work," Helen told her daughter-in-law. "You'll notice that Bertha and I are going to be there more than the others, so prepare yourself now to only see the little prince or princess when it's time to eat."

A voice spoke from the entryway. "Why don't you think I can take care of my wife and child?" All of the ladies turned toward the living room door and looked at Xavier, back to check on his wife. Again.

He walked over to the lounge chair and stooped to look into Bailey's face. "Are you feeling alright?" When she nodded her head, he stood and looked at each of the ladies. "I can take care of my wife and our baby just fine, thank you," he said and walked out of the room.

Victoria said, "If we are going to do some girl talk, we better get started before he comes back. He's here every half hour, you know."

The ladies all laughed, and Kendra added, "Don't worry, girl. When the next one is on the way, he won't even think to get you a glass of water. So enjoy the attention now."

After getting her back in their home and settled in bed, Xavier asked Bailey if she wanted something to eat. She answered, "No, Xavier, I don't want a fried onion and ketchup sandwich, and neither do you. You've got to stop eating like that. You know it makes you sick. Remember that vanilla ice cream and green olive milkshake you had last Friday?" When he nodded his head and looked at her sheepishly, she continued. "Then you should remember that you were in bed all weekend with an upset stomach after that horrible concoction."

They both had a good laugh, and he climbed into the bed behind her so they could practice breathing exercises. When the exercise session ended, Bailey leaned back on her husband's chest with her eyes closed, enjoying him caressing her extended abdomen.

"Bailey, the baby's kicking!" he exclaimed. "Does it hurt when the little cherub moves like that?"

She shook her head. "Not really. It's just a little uncomfortable sometimes, but I enjoy it. It lets me know that our baby is healthy and active." She wiped a tear as it rolled down her cheek.

Knowing she was emotional, Xavier kissed the top of her head, massaged her back, then pulled her to his chest and rubbed her belly until she fell asleep.

HOW

* * *

Monday morning dawned clear and bright, but Bailey was not her usual cheerful self. This was her last day of work at Jackson and Monroe. She was enjoying the baby shower even though the thought of leaving carried some bittersweet feelings.

"Miss Bailey, I'm going to miss you," Ja'Nell said tearfully.

"I know you won't be back for a while, so I'll be out to see you from time to time," Marie said, hugging her friend.

Alexander Jackson's wife and son, Melody and Alex Jr., were at the farewell shower too. As Melody hugged Bailey, she said to her, "There's nothing better than staying home to raise your child yourself, Bailey. Think about that." She smiled at Bailey and then winked at her.

Chapter 46: It's Time

"Where have you been? What are you doing?" Xavier asked his wife as she stepped into the house, closed the front door, maneuvered the three steps from the entry hall, and waddled her way across the living room floor.

"Trying to find a comfortable chair to sit in," she said. "I just finished my walk. What are you doing home so early?"

"I came home to be with you. I had a strong desire to see my beautiful wife, and you weren't here."

Bailey went to the armchair where Xavier was and sat on his lap.

"Oof!" Xavier grunted playfully with a gleaming smile. "You're going to make my legs go to sleep." When Bailey laughed and playfully slapped his shoulder, he tilted her back and kissed her, caressing her abdomen. He frowned. "Bailey, your tummy feels awfully tight, are you okay?"

"You say that every time you rub my belly, silly," she said. "Don't you remember? The doctor said any day now at our last weekly checkup. Besides, I just finished my daily walk and the little one is probably tired from all that exercise. Now come on up and help me take my shower. My back hurts a little. I guess I'm rather tired myself."

Bailey had just gotten her nightgown over her head when she felt pressure at the base of her abdomen, some light cramping, and then she felt a little pop. "Xavier," she said softly, "I need you to do something for me, please."

Xavier was sitting in the recliner watching television. "What can I do for you, sexy?"

"Call the doctor," she said, "then help me downstairs and get me to the hospital. My water just broke."

* * *

Bertha arrived at the hospital just after Bailey was connected to the fetal heart monitor. She kissed her daughter on the cheek and looked at her son-in-law. "Xavier, are you sick? Why do you look like that?"

Bailey gave a weak smile. "Mom, I just had a really strong contraction, and I don't think he was ready to see that."

"Xavier, women have been having babies since time began. Relax, she's going to be alright," Bertha said.

When the rest of the family arrived and filled the waiting room, Bertha joined them and gave everyone an update. "She's doing fine. The doctor said it could be as much as twelve hours. But I hope it's going to be a shorter labor. I don't think Xavier can hold on for that long."

The monitor began to beep faster as the contractions increased, and the father-to-be was right there beside his wife, coaching and soothing her through it. He wiped her brow and mopped the tears from her eyes. "Relax, sweetheart, you did well with that one. Take the refreshing breaths, close your eyes and I'll massage your back."

Xavier was glad that she closed her eyes. He didn't want her to see the strain and fear on his face. He thought, *I love this woman now more than I have ever loved her.* He kissed her neck as he was kneading her back and shoulders and whispered into her ear, "I love you. You're going to be a wonderful mommy."

She was so tired—tired of pushing, tired of hurting. If Xavier hadn't been there encouraging her along the way, she would have given up and told the doctor to just take the baby. But he was right there beside her.

"Come on, Bailey, you can do it! Do what the doctor asks. Take a deep breath and give a couple more pushes."

And that was what she did. After another fifteen minutes, the doctor said, "Okay, Bailey, you can rest, and we'll let you and this handsome little boy get to know each other." The doctor gently laid the newborn on her chest.

Xavier was excited as he cut the umbilical cord and heard his son's first cries. Then he watched the baby go through the cleanup process. Finally, he signed the permission for the circumcision and knew that after a few minutes, the little man was going to be delivered back to the new mother so they could continue bonding.

Standing by the bed looking at his wife as she was feeding their son, Xavier couldn't resist kissing her and the baby. "Thank you, Bailey, for being my wife, and for giving me this beautiful baby," he said softly.

"Zachary Anderson Monroe was born twenty-seven minutes ago weighing nine pounds, 1.5 ounces, and he's twenty-three-and-a-half inches long!" the proud father announced to the family gathered in the waiting room. "Mother and baby are doing fine."

Epilogue

When mother and baby made it home, the house was full of relatives. Everyone wanted to see the newest Monroe up close and personal. Bailey was led to the large recliner, and baby Zachary was held and cooed over by the grandparents.

While the ladies remained in the great room, the men went out onto the deck off the family room, where cigars and bottles of beer were passed out. Xavier was patted on the back by the brothers and brothers-in-law.

"Congratulations, Xavier, today you are a man," Caleb said, handing Xavier a cigar. "We understand that you made it through the birth without fainting once. We're so proud of you, man." When the laughter faded, Clayton held his beer up and led the toast. "To the newest father in the family. Congrats, little brother. If you ever need any advice about fatherhood, just come to the expert, and that would be Dad, of course."

Laughing and nodding their heads, they all touched bottles, drank their beers, and patted the new father on his back.

After two hours, Xavier returned to the great room and helped Bailey from her chair, took the baby from the bassinet, and walked them both up the steps into the bedroom. As soon as mother and baby were settled, Xavier leaned down and kissed his wife. She looked at him, beaming with happiness.

Easily returning her smile, Xavier reached into his pocket and pulled out a small velvet drawstring bag. "Thank you for our son, and for two interesting years," he said and gently sat on the edge of the bed, looking deeply into his wife's eyes.

Bailey returned his gaze and saw the tears beginning to well up in his eyes. Reaching out, she cupped her husband's face in her hands. Softly she said, "Xavier, I owe you an apology for the way I reacted to the order of dissolution, but I didn't know what else to do."

When he started to say something, she kissed him.

"No, let me finish," she said. He nodded his head, and she continued. "I realized that I was hopelessly in love with you, and I didn't know if you felt the same way about me or not. I didn't want to burden you with an unplanned child, so I left and tried to forget about you, but I couldn't. I was so sad and lonely. I didn't know what I was going to do, and when you showed up at the hospital, that was one of the happiest days of my life. I love you beyond measure, Xavier Monroe."

Overwhelmed with emotion, Xavier affectionately replied, "I hope that by now you know that I love you. I have to admit that I thought I was going to lose my mind if I lost you. And then when I found out that we were expecting, I knew I had to get you back in my life. I didn't want to live the rest of my life without you."

Trying to regain control, he cleared his throat and gently handed his wife the soft black bag. Bailey opened the pouch and emptied its contents into her hand. It was her platinum chain necklace, and Xavier had added another pearl with another set of teardrop diamonds on each side.

She looked at him and smiled. "Xavier, this is beautiful. You didn't have to do this, but I appreciate it."

"This is my way of saying to you that I thought you were the most beautiful expectant mother I'd ever seen, and now you are the most beautiful new mother I've ever seen. And I intend to add another pearl every year to this chain for the next fifty or sixty years to show you my lasting love and affection."

After he leaned forward and fastened the chain around her neck, Xavier stood and walked to the bedroom door. Holding the doorknob, he turned to look at his wife and son.

"Are you coming back, soon, Daddy?" Bailey asked.

"Yes," he said, "as soon as I can. You get some rest while the little man's asleep, and I'll get rid of all those people downstairs. Then I'll be back. While I'm gone, just remember that I love you madly, both of you."

As her husband and the father of their child left the room, Bailey smiled to herself and whispered, "I don't care how I got into this relationship with you, Xavier. I'm just glad I did."

About the Author

G. Louise Beard was born in Baltimore, Maryland. The second of five children, she earned a B.S. in Special Education from Coppin State College. She and her family relocated to Ogden, Utah, where she earned an M.Ed. in Secondary Education from Weber State University.

An avid reader, she spent her early years dreaming of becoming a writer, however, the necessities of life—marriage, raising a family, teaching, and becoming a minister/pastor's wife—took priority and kept the dream at bay.

Now in retirement, she is taking advantage of the opportunity to fulfill her dream of becoming a published author. She is the author of the books *Right Next Door*, *Mail Ordered*, *Nightmare*, and *How*. Visit www.glouisebeard.com for more information.